Just One Taste

A Kingston Family Dirty Dare Story

NEW YORK TIMES BESTSELLING AUTHOR

Carly Phillips

Print Edition

Cover Photo: Wander Aguiar
Cover Design: Maria @steamydesigns

* * *

Chapter One

NICOLETTE BETTENCOURT WOKE up and reached for her cell phone. She set the ringer and notifications on silent at night and checked her email and texts first thing in the morning. As soon as she turned on her phone, the messages and notifications popped up so fast she couldn't keep up.

She pushed herself up and focused on a message from her modeling agent, Amelia Mitchell: *Open this and call me immediately. You're all over the internet.*

Nikki looked at the link to the biggest tabloid site, one known for breaking the hottest stories in celebrity and entertainment news, and her stomach pitched. Whatever it was, it couldn't be good.

She clicked and studied the photo on the screen, trying to process what she saw. It was her bedroom, with the familiar chandelier hanging from the ceiling, the twin floral framed photos on the wall above the headboard, and the domed smart light on the right nightstand because Nikki found it difficult to wake up on workdays. *What the hell?*

Her pale pink duvet lay rumpled on one side of the bed, and then she took in the part she'd avoided looking at until now, the female lying asleep on the other side. Nikki tried but found it impossible to swallow. Heart pounding, she enlarged the picture, even though she already knew. *She* was the girl naked in bed, her ass exposed for the world to see. *But how?*

Nauseous, she scrolled lower only to find another photo of herself, her hair pulled up into a messy bun, her face visible as she slept on her back. Censorship bars covered her private parts but she was naked nonetheless. Shame washed over her and she started to tremble.

How had someone taken photos of her in her own home? Tears filled her eyes, and she glanced down at her *nude* body—because that's how she slept… when she slept—and freaked out. She jumped out of bed, grabbed the silk robe slung over the footboard, and wrapped the material around herself, shaking as she tied the sash tight around her waist.

She felt exposed, violated, and utterly petrified.

She wasn't ready to talk to her agent or anyone else for that matter. She scrolled through her phone, seeing her mother had called no less than a dozen times. Her parents would be furious, worried about how this would impact her senator father's potential presidential campaign.

Any other twenty-one-year-old girl would call a friend, but Nikki didn't have anyone she trusted completely. The closest person to her was Megan Cologne, another model. But Meg wasn't the warm-fuzzy type, and Nikki needed someone to comfort her, not gloat. Meg was the gloating type.

Her doorbell rang and she froze. She couldn't face anyone. Not now. Then she remembered the doorman would only let a select few people come up without calling. People she could handle seeing.

Pulling her robe tighter, she walked into the main area of her apartment and tiptoed to the door.

Someone banged again and rang the bell. "Come on, Nikki. Let me in."

She let out a breath of relief and opened the door. "Derek!" She fell into her big brother's arms, not bothering to hold back choking sobs.

"Come on." He wrapped an arm around her and walked them inside, shutting the door and locking it behind them. "I don't have to ask if you're okay but how did this happen? How were pictures like that taken and exposed?"

She pushed herself out of his embrace. "I don't know, okay? I admit I sleep naked but nobody's been here!"

"No guys? Boyfriends or otherwise?" he asked.

She shook her head. "Not since Lance Freeman. That was six months ago." Her ex-boyfriend was a photographer she'd met through her modeling career.

They'd been casual, and Nikki always had a hunch he'd been with her for the wrong reasons. Namely her family name and modeling connections. But she'd been lonely and he'd been there. Eventually, they'd argued more often than not and she broke up with him. He'd seemed to agree it was over and that was that.

"I'll be right back." She rushed to the bathroom and grabbed some tissues, blotting her eyes and wetting her face before rejoining her brother in the family room.

"Have you spoken to Lance lately?"

"No. I ended things and it was as amicable as a breakup could be." She lifted her shoulders. "That was it. I swear to you I have no idea how anyone got in here while I was sleeping. And that had to be what happened, right?" She shivered at the possibility.

Derek's scowl would scare anyone except her. Nikki knew he wasn't angry at her, he was pissed at the situation and worried. "I'll figure that part out."

Her phone rang from the bedroom and she groaned. "Mom's been calling nonstop. So has my agent. I didn't look to see who else left messages. I just know I've been slammed with notifications, too. I don't want to deal with any of it." She grew queasy at the thought of people viewing those photos, yet she knew half the world had seen them by now. God, what if the pictures had been uploaded somewhere without the black bars covering her most private parts? What if she was truly naked online for the world to see? Nausea filled her at the violation that was even worse than the fact that Senator Corbin Bettencourt's daughter was in the headlines again.

Derek put a calming hand on her shoulder. "Go get your phone and call Mom while I'm here. Then we'll figure out our next move."

Knowing he was right, she nodded. She walked to her room and picked up her cell, suddenly uncomfortable being in the bedroom that had always been her comfort space.

She returned to Derek, who'd taken or made a phone call of his own.

Her cell rang again and *Mom* showed up on the screen. "Might as well get it over with," she muttered. Drawing a deep breath, she took the call. "Hello?"

"Nicolette Anne," her mother cried out, her voice shrill, as she used the longer, proper name her parents preferred, refusing to call her Nikki, the shortened version *she'd* chosen. "How could you let such a thing happen? Do you have any idea how mortifying this is for your father and me?"

What about what how awful it is for me? Nikki wondered, not voicing the thought out loud. Her mother wouldn't care. Thank God she had Derek by her side and always had.

Seeing he'd put a hand to his ear to block her voice while he spoke on his phone, she took a few steps away so they could each hear their respective callers.

"It's not like I posed for the photo, Mother. Someone somehow took pictures of me when I was sleeping. They violated my privacy!"

"Come now. Do you really think I believe such a thing? You've constantly disappointed us. Between your grades in school and the issues with being on time for modeling shoots, your name in the papers when your contract details leaked–"

Nikki blinked, hating the tears her mother managed to bring out so easily. Normally she tried to be immune to the *you're a disappointment* theme, but she was in a vulnerable place and her mother was using it against her.

"There were legitimate reasons for those things, too," Nikki reminded her mother. But heaven forbid Collette Bettencourt acknowledged her daughter's issues.

Nikki had inherited dyslexia from her mother's side of the family, since her uncle suffered from it as well, and Nikki's inability to read well had resulted in poor grades in school. Her mother had never allowed tutors because nobody could find out Nicolette wasn't perfect.

"Nicolette, are you listening?" her mother asked, her annoyed tone one Nikki was used to hearing.

"I'm here."

Her mother had been asking how they were going to explain naked pictures of their daughter to the press and digging in on what an embarrassment Nicolette was to the family. She'd tuned her mother out.

"I'm not interested in anything but making this go away. Who took the pictures?" her mother asked.

"I told you, I don't know."

Derek finished his call, slipped his phone into his pants pocket, and walked over, holding out his arm, palm up.

Nikki handed him the phone, their mother's tone loud as her complaining continued.

"Mother."

At the sound of Derek's voice, Collette stopped her berating and changed her inflection. "Derek, honey, please help us. Your sister–"

"Is in trouble, or don't you care? Her privacy has been violated, she's scared to death, and all you can think about is Dad's career. If you can't find compassion for your daughter, leave her alone. Goodbye, Mother." He disconnected the call and turned to Nikki. "Now that's taken care of. Let's talk."

Although there'd been a time Derek was more amenable to their mother's needs and demands, after a broken engagement with a woman their mother had insisted was perfect for him, he'd taken a stand. Derek was his own man. Not that it stopped their mother from trying to manipulate him.

Nodding, Nikki followed him into the kitchen. In a daze, she made them coffee, finding the chore of doing something routine helpful in calming her nerves.

After she'd put milk and sugar on the table and joined him, they each doctored their morning brew.

Derek met her gaze. "The paparazzi are going to swarm outside the building soon, if they haven't already. I'd like to get you out of here."

Her stomach twisted at the thought. "And go where?"

Derek reached out and covered her hand with his. "I have an idea but you need to trust me. I'm going to talk to Asher," he said of his close friend.

Asher Dare was a sexy, brooding man she barely knew, but she recalled making an awful impression on him when they'd met. She'd been seventeen, coming home from a rough photo shoot in Mexico, tired, miserable, and so ready to get home when a customs agent pulled her over thanks to a medication bottle found in her bag. Nobody believed she hadn't bought the drugs herself, that she'd been set up. Flashes of being arrested had gone through her mind during the questioning, and panic had engulfed her.

By the time her father's team had done their magic and gotten her out of there, she'd been sweaty, had had to pee for hours, and her mother's yelling over the phone had upset her even more. Neither of her parents had picked her up after her ordeal. No doubt her mother had refused to come or let her father show his face – in case the media had caught on to the story. Her mother was the force behind the senator, and he caved to her demands.

Derek had picked her up and Asher had been with him. She admitted now that she'd been obnoxious and probably rude, but after what she'd been through, it was a miracle she hadn't collapsed into a puddle on the floor. But Asher's initial impression of her hadn't been good a good one.

She sighed. "Why talk to Asher?" she asked her brother.

"He has an estate on Windermere Island. It's off Eleuthera, near the Bahamas. You can lie low until something else takes over the news cycle. You'll be safe and no one will think to look for you there."

"Will you come with me?" she asked.

Derek squeezed her hand. "I wish I could, but I have a closing this week."

"Oh, right." Derek's company, Blackout Media, was purchasing a start-up social media group he planned to incorporate into his conglomerate. She didn't want to make him feel any worse, so she forced a small smile. "Okay. If you think that's best."

He nodded. "I do. If Asher agrees, I'll be back to take you to his private jet. Can you pack while I'm gone?"

She hated the idea of going away alone right now. "Are you sure I need to leave?"

Derek rose and walked over, bracing an arm around her shoulder. "Would you rather stay in Manhattan until things die down and we figure out who did this?"

Her eyes filled again. The thought of staying in her home, where *it* had happened, was more terrifying. "No."

He rose to his full height. "I'll be back as soon as I can. Meanwhile, you're safe here. Not only did I put the fear of God into Preston at the desk downstairs, but I have a bodyguard hanging around incognito on the front sidewalk and another out back. Nobody's getting into the building who doesn't belong."

They both knew her father ought to be the one to hire security for his daughter. He was the parent. It wasn't Derek's responsibility, but here he was, stepping up. As always. He'd been twelve when she was born and had been an amazing big brother. When her sleep issues kicked in, he'd been there, letting her use a sleeping bag in his room every time thunder and lightning struck or if she couldn't get her brain to shut off. Even if she tossed and turned, Derek's presence had always calmed her.

"Love you," she said.

"Love you, too, peanut."

He used the nickname he'd chosen as she was growing up and she groaned. "Don't call me that."

He reached out and tweaked her nose with his thumb and forefinger, another holdout from when she was a kid. "I'll be back. Don't let anyone in you don't know."

Nodding, she walked him to the door and locked up behind him.

★ ★ ★

AFTER RECEIVING A call from Derek Bettencourt, a business school buddy and good friend, Asher left a family barbecue early to meet him at Asher's office. Derek's younger sister, Nicolette, had gotten herself into another situation that required fixing. Compromising photos were splashed all over the internet, and Asher winced, knowing if it had been his sister, he'd want to kill someone. If Derek wanted to stash Nicolette at Asher's island home until things blew over, that was fine with him.

He recalled meeting Nicolette when she was seventeen and he'd gone with Derek to pick her up at the airport. She'd been late, and it had taken a ridiculous amount of time to find out she'd been caught by customs with illegal drugs in her bag.

She'd sworn someone had set her up. Derek had believed her. The senator and his wife had not. Asher, who'd already had a bad experience dating a model, was inclined to agree with the elder Bettencourts.

Asher's ex had been a model with a big-name agency. Christy been doing well for herself. She was gorgeous, which, in his mid-twenties, had been a huge bonus. Over time, he'd learned she was flighty, consistently late for important events, and too self-centered for his liking. But she'd looked good on his arm, had been great in bed, and he'd been shallow enough to ignore the warning signs of trouble. He'd even given her a key to his apartment, which, by the end of their relationship, they were basically sharing.

He'd left work early to surprise her, something he rarely did, and came home to find cocaine spread over the table in the living area and Christy in his bed with her new yoga trainer. A flexible guy if their position had been any indication. He thought he'd been in love, though he knew better now. She'd been the second and last woman to break his heart. From then on, he'd thrown himself into short-term flings where the women knew not to expect more than sex.

As he turned into the parking garage, Asher acknowledged that his vision of Nicolette was skewed. Her behavior had brought back bad memories of Christy but he was still inclined to err on the side of caution when it came to Derek's sister.

Asher pulled into a parking spot below the Dirty Dare Spirits offices in Midtown West. The company and the property were owned by Asher and his siblings, but he ran the business. As it was a long July Fourth weekend, the building was quiet.

The interior design consisted of four bars spread out on the ground level. Each served a variety of coffee and alcohol, depending on the time of day. A separate floor held a lab where mixologists created craft cocktails, and the office space was on the floors above.

He took the elevator from the underground garage to the main level, stepped out, and walked toward the front entrance. Derek was waiting outside and the security guard had yet to notice him. The building was locked on the weekends and Asher strode over to let his friend in.

Asher greeted Derek with a brotherly hug and pat on the back.

"Thanks for coming. I figured this place was the easiest for us to meet." Derek ran a hand through his already mussed jet-black hair, a sure sign he had a lot on his mind.

"No problem. Let's go upstairs and talk. Want coffee?" Asher offered. The coffee bars were closed but he could make them drinks.

Derek shook his head. "I'm wired enough already. Thanks."

They started to walk toward the elevators, and Asher nodded at the weekend guard. "Hi, Tim. Good holiday weekend with the family?"

The older man, who'd worked there prior to Asher buying the building, nodded. "We had our barbecue yesterday. Thanks for asking, Mr. Dare."

Asher smiled. "Have a good one."

He and Derek took the elevator to his office floor. Once inside, Asher turned on the light. They settled into the comfortable chairs in the corner across from his desk, and Asher waited for Derek to talk.

"You've seen the photos?" Derek finally asked.

Not wanting to make things worse, Asher said, "Just a glimpse."

"But enough to know what we're dealing with."

"Yeah. Is your father livid?" Asher said.

"Haven't heard from him but my mother sure as hell is." Derek's expression grew furious, his mouth turning downward in a scowl. "And not for the reasons she should be. As usual, she's concerned with dad's reputation. I'm worried about my sister. Somehow, someone got into her apartment to take those photographs, and she's a mess. Scared, embarrassed, you name it. I'm not sure there are enough words to cover it."

Asher winced. Jade was right. He'd been judgmental without knowing the facts. Still, once again, Nicolette was in trouble that she claimed someone else had caused.

He got right to the point. "So, you want to send your sister to my island house?" A place he'd purchased once Dirty Dare Vodka, as it was then known, had succeeded. His getaway had become a family escape.

Derek nodded. "I know it's a big ask, but I need to get Nikki out of town until things blow over in the press. It'll also give me time to have someone figure out when and how those photos were taken."

Asher met his friend's gaze. "No problem. But we didn't need to meet in person. I'd have said yes over the phone. What's going on?"

Derek steepled his fingers, his gaze steady on Asher's. "I want you to go with her and stay so she's not alone."

Asher blinked in shock. "Seriously? Why don't *you* take her? I'm sure she'd be more comfortable with her brother than someone she barely knows."

Inclining his head, Derek groaned. "You're right

and I would, but I have a deal closing this week."

"Shit. Does she want to go with a friend?" Asher wouldn't mind letting two women use the guest rooms at his house. That way he could do his friend a favor and avoid babysitting a woman with a penchant for finding trouble. One who reminded him of his own bad choices.

Derek shook his head. "Our family name makes it hard for her to trust. People in the modeling industry think she got where she is because of connections. There have been a number of incidents over the years in both social media and the news that make her look bad."

Asher kept his opinion to himself.

Derek leaned forward. "Listen, I wouldn't ask if I didn't really need the favor. I can't send her alone, she's too shaken up, and I *trust* you."

Asher pinched the bridge of his nose. He didn't have any pressing business coming up, but he wasn't a good choice to be Derek's sister's companion. They had nothing in common, not to mention, Asher wasn't sure she was as innocent as her brother believed. Not with the way she jet setted across the world and the fast crowd he'd seen photos of her running with.

"I didn't want to do this," Derek said in the wake of Asher's silence. "But remember the stage-five clinger you couldn't shake? *You owe me.*"

Asher groaned. After Christy, he'd tried to be selective and not get into long-term relationships. The woman Derek mentioned though? She'd been impossible to get rid of despite the fact that he'd been blunt up front. He hadn't been looking for anything but fun in bed.

At first, he'd tried being pleasant, but she wouldn't take a hint and brought him lunch every day at work for a week until he'd had to tell the guard to turn her away. She'd shown up outside his apartment each time he went to the gym, and he'd had to change his schedule. He had no idea how she'd known where he lived or what his plans were until he'd discovered she'd befriended his personal assistant, who had shared his information. Then he'd had two women to get rid of.

Asher had been at his favorite upscale bar with Derek, and she'd arrived uninvited. Apparently, she'd decided the best way to get Asher's attention was to make him jealous, and she'd started hanging all over Derek.

"She sure as fuck transferred her affections easily enough and then she became *my* problem. I had to change my cell phone number and make out a police report," Derek muttered.

The man had a point. Asher did owe him. Besides, he'd been about to agree anyway, because he valued the other man's friendship. "Okay. I was just wrapping my head around the idea of taking Nicolette to the island."

"She likes to be called Nikki. Only my parents call her Nicolette."

"And the media," Asher said, but once they reached the hangar where his plane was, they wouldn't have to worry about the paps.

"Thank you." Derek slapped him on the back. "There are only a handful of friends I trust with my baby sister, and you're one of them. Plus, you have a house on an island," he said with a chuckle. "Look at it this way. This time I owe *you* one."

"It's no problem," Asher lied.

"I'll bring Nikki to Teterboro," Derek said of the private airport where Asher kept his jet.

Asher nodded, wondering how the hell he'd handle being alone with a twenty-one-year-old girl with a diva-like reputation, who'd no doubt been pampered throughout her life. Even if spoiling her seemed to be a way for her parents to keep her at a distance. Knowing what it was like to have a close family, he felt a tug of conscience for what Nikki had been through, but at least she'd had her brother.

Asher would give anything for Derek to have chosen someone else for this job, but as he'd pointed out, Asher had the home on the island. And a promise was a promise. Even if this trip was guaranteed to be the longest of his life.

Chapter Two

WHILE NIKKI PACKED for the beach and waited for Derek to return, her cell phone rang. Wary, she glanced at the device, seeing the one friend she had in the modeling world's name flash on the screen.

She answered on the second ring. "Hi, Meg."

"Girl, what is going on with you?" Meg yelled into the phone. "The whole world has seen your ass."

Nikki winced. Though Meg could be crass and blunt, she was the only one nice to Nikki when they were surrounded by other models. The rest had labeled Nikki a diva, and her life on the runway was basically a version of *Mean Girls*. More and more, Nikki wanted out of the life she'd chosen out of necessity, but now wasn't the time to think that far into the future.

"Can you not remind me about what the world has seen?" Paranoid, she looked around her bedroom and pulled down the shade.

"Don't worry about anything. Knowing you, you'll make lemonade out of this mess."

Nikki rolled her eyes and packed a few more bathing suits. "You seem to think my life is charmed. I can assure you it's not."

Meg snorted and Nikki ignored the sound. Meg went on discussing the mean comments on the sites showing the photos, all the while assuring Nikki things would pass. The beautiful blonde had grown up poor and arrived in Manhattan with nothing more than a backpack and a dream of being a model. She'd chosen the last name, Cologne, for her career, hoping it would make her stand out. Nikki considered Meg lucky she hadn't met the wrong person before finding a job at an independent clothing store whose owner had friends in the right places.

A knock sounded on her door and Nikki froze. "I have to go."

"Call me and tell me what you plan on doing about this mess," Meg said before Nikki disconnected the call.

She tiptoed to her door and peeked through the peephole, to see it was her upstairs neighbor Winter Capwell, with her dog, Panda, a black and white Havanese, by her side. Although Nikki didn't know Winter well, they'd run into one another coming in and out of the building, and in the gym on the top floor. They'd exchanged numbers last week, agreeing to go for coffee one day soon.

Winter was a journalist, which immediately put Nikki on edge, and she hadn't reached out to her as a friend for that reason alone. So far, all they'd talked about were streaming shows, books, and how much they both loved dogs. Nothing to set off alarm bells, but there was always the chance that Winter's interest in friendship was really an attempt to get close to Nikki for *other* reasons. With Nikki's sudden notoriety, she worried the other woman had a hidden agenda for showing up now.

Nikki kept the chain on and opened the door. "Hi," she said, glancing at her neighbor.

Winter was dressed in workout clothes, tight leggings and a cropped top, her long dark hair, similar to Nikki's, in a ponytail. She was probably coming from or heading out for a dog walk.

"What's up?" Nikki asked.

Winter's eyes softened as she took in Nikki's obviously wary gaze.

"You saw the photos?" she asked. Because why else would Winter be here?

The other woman nodded. "I thought maybe you wanted company?"

"Really?" Nikki asked, her sarcasm heavy.

"Honestly. Off the record. Nothing you say will go beyond us. I just thought maybe you could use a friend."

Winter's warm tone and honest expression got to her. The sweet gesture caused Nikki's eyes to fill with unexpected tears. With that one sentence, Winter was kinder than her friend Meg had been.

Nikki undid the chain and stepped aside. “Come on in.”

Winter walked inside and Nikki locked the door again. “I’m sorry if I’m acting weird. I have trouble trusting people right now.”

“I understand, believe me.”

Nikki dropped down and petted the fluffy dog’s head. “How are you, Panda?”

The dog rolled over for a belly rub.

“We were going out for a walk when I decided to stop by,” Winter said.

Nikki rose and she led Winter to the sofa. They sat down beside each other, and Panda lay at her owner’s feet.

“Listen, I get that things are hard right now but it’ll blow over. These things always do.” Winter spoke with certainty.

“Thank you. I hope so.” Nikki wasn’t going to get into details about the photos or her fear. For one thing, she was still wary of giving a journalist information. And for another, there was no sense freaking out her neighbor about someone getting into her apartment.

“Is your family upset?” Winter asked.

Nikki narrowed her gaze. “Why are you asking?”

Winter sighed. "I didn't mean anything by the question. *Most* parents would be worried about their children if someone tried to exploit them."

Nikki shook her head. "You're right. Sorry I jumped to conclusions." Was it any wonder she didn't have any good friends? Her brother had his tight-knit group of guys and she envied their closeness. No ulterior motives to be found. "I'm just tense."

"Can I make you a cup of tea?" Winter offered.

Nikki shook her head and glanced down at her shaking hands. "I had coffee. That was obviously a mistake. What story are you currently working on?" she asked, eager to change the subject.

"I'm interviewing the partners of K-Talent Productions, Sasha and Xander Kingston, Cassidy Kingston, who's taken on a bigger role, and Harrison Dare. As relatively new as they are to the movie and production business, they're racking up awards and accolades. And their female-centric focus is of particular interest to me."

Intrigued by the subject matter, Nikki leaned forward. "Really? I find the intricacies of what happens behind the scenes on a movie set fascinating. I wish I could learn more."

It seemed more exciting than walking down a runway and showing off designer clothes. Not that she was knocking the career she'd been fortunate to cultivate so young in life or the other girls who loved it. Nikki was just interested in finding something different. Something more.

A rap sounded and she jumped, as did Panda. The dog began to bark and Winter shushed her. Nikki walked to the door and glanced through the peephole again.

"Derek," she said, relieved. "It's my brother." She undid the locks again and Derek strode past her. "Did I hear a… dog?" His eyes fell to Winter and Panda.

"Derek, this is my neighbor, Winter Capwell. Winter, my brother, Derek Bettencourt."

He narrowed his gaze. "I thought I said not to let anyone in?"

"You said no one I didn't know. I know Winter."

Winter's smile was tight. "It's nice to meet you. I'm glad you're looking out for your sister. I'm going to take the dog for her walk. Take care, Nikki. I'll check on you soon."

Nikki nodded. "Thanks for stopping by."

Derek walked Winter out and locked up again before turning to Nikki.

She held up a hand. "Please don't give me a hard time. She stopped by as a friend, and I could use one of those right now."

His eyes softened in understanding. "I know. I didn't expect to see anyone here. Are you packed?"

She nodded. "I just have to put a few things in my toiletry bag." Thanks to the travel involved in her career, she always had a cosmetic kit ready to go. "I take it Asher agreed to let me stay at his house?"

Derek put a hand on her back and they walked to her bedroom. "It took some convincing but he's meeting us at the airport. He'll take you to the island and stay with you until it's time for you to come home."

"What?" Nikki spun around to face her brother. "You can't be serious. I don't know him and I'll feel like I'm invading his space."

It was Derek's turn to hold up a hand, pushing off her objection. "I still don't believe anyone will figure out where you are, but I'll feel better knowing you won't be alone. I trust him. Asher knows his staff, and he'll be aware if anyone sneaks onto the property who isn't allowed. Do this for me?"

She frowned but couldn't say no. Not after her brother had gone to the trouble to arrange this getaway for her safety.

"Look at it this way. Mom and Dad won't know where you are either." His lips lifted in a smirk, and she couldn't help but laugh, too.

"Okay. I'll do it for you. Because you're the best brother, Derek. Seriously."

Nikki then left a message for her agent that she

was disappearing until things blew over, only telling her she'd be in touch when she was ready. There was no one else she needed to call. She finished packing and they took the private elevator downstairs to the garage where he'd parked his car.

At Derek's direction, she lay down on the back seat, so when he pulled out of the parking garage, none of the paparazzi lurking with cameras could see her. He waited until he was certain they weren't followed before telling her she could sit up.

On the ride to the airport, she remained silent, her thoughts consumed with her soon-to-be host. She was well aware the man probably had to be talked into staying with her on the island. His most recent dealing with her had been years ago, but she'd been hysterical after being detained by airport security and customs agents, her mother's yelling had been ringing in her ear, and she'd been a bitch to both Asher and Derek. She'd never seen him again to apologize, and it was way too late to bring it up now.

Yet Derek had asked him to drop everything and *babysit* her because she'd ended up with naked photos splashed on the internet. She cringed at what Asher probably thought of her. As they pulled into the airport hangar, she could add one more word to describe what she was feeling.

Nervous to face Asher Dare.

★ ★ ★

ASHER STOOD IN the airplane hangar and checked his watch, a Patek Philippe Mariner he'd purchased when he'd made his first million on his own, without the family hotel business income included. Derek and his sister should arrive any minute, and he braced himself for the week to come. With any luck, she was a sunbather who'd enjoy the beach, prefer solitude, and leave him to work and do his own thing.

Escorting her around the nearby town and sharing meals could get awkward. What did he have in common with a twenty-one year-old?

His cell rang, and seeing it was his brother, Harrison, he answered the call. "Hello?"

"Hey," Harrison said. "I just got to Mom and Dad's and they said you took off. Sorry I missed you."

"I had to go meet a friend who needed a favor," Asher said as Derek's black Porsche SUV pulled in. "I'm headed to the island for a while."

Nicolette stepped out of the SUV, and Asher expelled a sharp breath at the sight of the long legs in high heels that hit his vision first, followed by a black miniskirt and a royal-blue tight, cropped top that accentuated her full breasts. His gaze traveled to her face, and despite her eyes being covered by large sunglasses, he knew she was beautiful.

Last time he'd seen her had been four years ago. He'd scrolled past the nude photos online today out of respect for his friend. But Nicolette's delicate features, olive skin, and gorgeous, long, silky dark hair took his breath away.

"Ash? You do remember we're coming in for the parents' anniversary this weekend, right?" Harrison asked.

Asher had forgotten his brother was on the phone. "Yeah," he muttered, not hearing a thing his sibling had said. "Gotta go. I'll call you later." He disconnected and slid his phone into his pants pocket.

Derek had lifted a Louis Vuitton suitcase from the back of the SUV and pulled it along with him as he and his sister approached. She stopped a few steps behind him.

"I can't thank you enough," Derek said, coming to a stop in front of him.

"It's fine," Asher assured him.

"Nikki, come meet Asher."

The beautiful brunette stepped beside her brother. "Nikki." Derek placed a hand on her back. "Do you remember my friend Asher?"

"It's been a while," she murmured, a blush staining her cheeks. Obviously she recalled their last time, too. "Thank you for helping me out."

"You're welcome." He inclined his head, studying

her from head to toe.

Did she always travel in fuck-me pumps? And why had he thought of *that* description? Now all he could imagine were those long legs wrapped around his hips as he did just that. To his friend's younger sister.

He would have to keep reminding himself how inappropriate sleeping with her would be. Assuming she would even be interested. He had first-hand knowledge of how awkward a large age gap could be. His father, Michael, had been thirty-four when he'd married Savannah, his stepmother. Between a seven-year age difference and the fact that she'd been the family nanny for nine years, the outside world assumed they'd been sleeping together all along.

At twelve years old, Asher had been too young to understand all the innuendo involved, but he sure as hell knew what teasing and bullying felt like. Even if the other kids were merely repeating things their parents had said, they'd meant to make fun of him and his family. To make him feel small and shitty. And they had. Michael and Serenity had been a scandal in their community, and Asher grew up wanting to avoid repeating the past.

If Asher and Nikki's twelve-year age-gap similarity didn't work to dull her sex appeal, he'd rely on his own morals and character. He wasn't willing to break Derek's trust, no matter how gorgeous and fuckable

Nikki might be.

Knowing he couldn't adjust his cock, discreetly or otherwise, he turned toward the plane. "You ready?" he asked, glancing over his shoulder to where she stood with her brother.

"Yes. I just need to say goodbye." She hugged Derek and they spoke in hushed tones.

Then her brother kissed her cheek and stepped back. "I'll talk to you every day, and I'll keep you up-to-date about what's going on. Stay off social media."

She cringed and nodded.

Matt, Asher's pilot ever since he'd purchased the jet, walked down the stairs and took the suitcase from beside Derek, returning to the plane to put it in the cargo hold. Jeremy, the co-pilot, was already on board.

Matt returned to where they stood. "Can I help you up the stairs?" he asked Nikki.

She smiled at him and nodded. "That's so kind of you."

Not liking how Matt looked at her, Asher sidled closer. "I've got her. We'll meet you on the plane," he said in an annoyed tone and immediately wondered what had gotten into him.

"Yes, Mr. Dare." Matt slid his hat between his body and arm and walked away.

Derek grinned. "I knew I could trust you to take care of my baby sister."

"I'm not a baby," she reminded him.

Asher didn't want to think of her as a woman. He'd have to find a way not to consider her any kind of sexual being. As hard as that would be given those full breasts and the sway of her hips as she'd confidently strode over to him.

Her sexy walk hadn't been intentional. He'd seen too many women using their wiles on a man, and Derek's sister, to his surprise, seemed unaware of her appeal. Modeling had obviously given her the tools to strut a runway, but her earlier blush had given away more of her true self. And wasn't that a refreshing surprise?

"Nicolette, ready to go?" Asher snapped at her, annoyed he was finding anything about her appealing.

She stiffened at his tone. "Call me Nikki, and yes, I'm ready."

Asher turned to his friend. "Don't worry about anything on our end. She'll be fine."

"Just concentrate on figuring out who did this to me," she said to Derek, her tone wounded and sad.

Asher swallowed hard. "Come on." He settled his hand on her lower back, trying and failing to ignore the heat coming from her body as he led her to the stairs.

They entered the jet designed by his cousin, Lucy Dare, who worked at the well-known firm of Mann &

Mann in Manhattan. Though Lucy had an ingrained fear of flying in small planes, she'd jumped at the chance to put her artistic stamp on the interior of his jet. He'd agreed, as long as she stuck to neutral colors. His Gulfstream could carry up to eighteen people, and considering how large Asher's family was, the size had been an important consideration.

"Take a seat," he said.

Nikki unknowingly walked to Asher's favorite chair and sat down, revealing even more thigh that had him drooling. She buckled herself in and met his gaze, obviously waiting for him to do the same.

He situated himself across from her, snapped on his seat belt, and picked up the bag Matt had already stored on board for him. If he had to go to the island, he'd use the flying time to get work done.

The plane doors closed and Nikki jerked at the sound. Obviously, she was nervous. About what part of this situation, Asher wasn't sure. All he knew was they were now alone, headed to his ocean paradise.

★ ★ ★

THE JET TOOK off and Nikki looked out the window, watching as the plane soared into the clouds, headed for an estate on an island with the quiet man sitting across from her, reading something on his tablet.

The interior was gorgeous, with plush leather seats in a deep cognac, with textured black accents on the headrest. The carpeting was equally luxurious. Each chair had a soft cashmere blanket folded and waiting for the passenger. After she'd finished admiring her surroundings, she looked in her bag for her phone, thinking she'd listen to music, but realized her messages and notifications would only upset her.

She tapped her feet on the floor and stared out the window. The longer she sat in silence while Asher studied whatever he was looking at on the screen, the more uncomfortable she became. Although he'd been a gentleman leading her onto the plane, he'd been snippy as well, and he'd cemented her gut feeling that he didn't want to be the one escorting her to his second home.

With him distracted, she studied him. She'd expected him to be in a suit and tie, the epitome of the uptight businessman, and she wasn't all wrong. He wasn't wearing a jacket, but he was in dress slacks and a white button-down shirt, sleeves rolled up, revealing tanned, muscular forearms. If he'd been wearing a tie earlier, he'd removed it and undone enough buttons to show his chest was also tan, with a sprinkling of hair showing through.

Nikki was used to guys with boyish appearances. Ones who had the toned, slim look the modeling agencies preferred, hair slicked back and overly styled. Asher Dare, with his closely trimmed beard and dark hair she was dying to run her fingers through, was all man.

She couldn't take the silence and cleared her throat. Since they were going to spend time together, she wanted to get to know him better.

He looked up from the screen, brows raised in curiosity, those intense, indigo eyes meeting hers, giving her a chance to see he had dark lashes most women would kill for.

She swallowed hard. "I wanted to say thank you for dropping everything to help me. I appreciate it."

"Your brother is a good friend. He asked and of course I said yes." His gaze shifted back down to his screen.

She continued to tap her toes on the floor, nervous energy flooding her. "What are you reading?"

He looked up again. "Competitive market research. I'm considering expanding, and I'm interested in the local brands sold, price parity, and whether we'd be welcomed since we're not a hometown brand." He stared at her for a beat, waiting for a reply.

She nodded. "That's… um… interesting."

"No, it's not." That got her the first lift of his lips in something that resembled a smile. A smile that changed the brooding hot male into a man with a sexy bad-boy smirk.

"Wouldn't you rather be reading the newest fashion magazine?" he asked.

She searched his expression and voice for snark at her profession and found none. "No. I need to stay off anything that might lead me to social media." She twisted her fingers in her lap as her cheeks no doubt flamed in embarrassment.

He winced. "I didn't mean to bring up a sore subject."

She shrugged. "Don't worry about it. But your reading material actually *is* interesting. I mean, would you potentially need a new bottle and design if you go into smaller markets? Or would your name and brand be enough to sell on?" She glanced at him and smiled. "See? Interesting."

He studied her, his expression hard to read. "Label change is an option in smaller markets," he acknowledged.

She did her best not to puff up with pride. "So how did you meet Derek?" she asked.

"He never mentioned it?"

She shook her head.

Asher lifted one leg and rested an ankle over his knee. "We shared a class our first year of business school. He, Knox, and I and another guy formed a study group. Three of us stayed close." Asher glanced back down at his tablet.

Nikki got the hint but she wanted to keep chatting. She *needed* to talk. If she engaged in conversation, she wouldn't think about why she was on this jet and heading out of town to begin with.

She bit down on the inside of her cheek. "What's your favorite color?" she asked.

He looked up again, his eyes crinkled in confusion. "Blue."

He didn't ask hers, though it was lavender. "Favorite movie?" she asked.

"We're really doing this?"

She nodded.

He sighed. "*The Godfather*."

"Ooh, blood and violence. Very manly so I'm not surprised." Again, he didn't ask hers, which was good since she didn't think he'd appreciate her answer, *Legally Blonde*. He already didn't take her seriously. "Favorite author?" She shifted in her seat.

"Baldacci." A muscle throbbed in his temple as she asked her next question, but he put up with her quizzing him for a while longer, and she'd gotten into a groove, losing count of how many fun get-to-know-you questions she'd tossed his way.

"Who do you admire most in the world?" she asked.

He worked his jaw back and forth. "I never

thought about it."

Hmm. What to ask next? Something light. Then, after his reply, she'd ask deeper questions, because despite his answers, he was still a sexy enigma to her. Something about his stoic short replies told her he was a man who held his emotions in check and didn't let many people close. He intrigued her and she wondered what more she could find out.

"How old were you when you stopped believing in Santa Claus?" she finally decided to ask.

He stared at her for a long moment, then pointed to the tablet. "Can you be quiet? I need to work," he said and returned to his silent reading.

She frowned at the rude comment and swallowed hard. "You could have asked nicely," she muttered.

He groaned loudly. "I really like your brother, but I didn't sign on for twenty questions. And to be frank, we're long past that number."

She ought to be insulted, but the truth was, her rambling often got on her brother's nerves and *he* loved her. Asher barely tolerated her.

"My rambling annoys Derek, too." Nikki kicked off her shoes and put her feet beneath her on the seat, getting more comfortable. "But he says *I love you* before he asks me to be quiet," she muttered under her breath.

"Still talking…"

She rolled her eyes, opened the butter-soft blanket, and covered herself. Then she grabbed a pillow with a large D monogrammed onto the case, curled up, and closed her eyes, knowing better than to think she'd nap. When she closed her eyes, those awful photos of her naked flickered through her anxiety-ridden mind, but she pretended to pass out so she wouldn't over-talk to Asher.

Chapter Three

Asher glanced at Nikki feigning sleep, her twitching body and soft, frustrated sighs giving her away. He'd been an asshole. To a woman going through her own trauma, which made him an even bigger dick. But he'd never been one to tolerate chitchat, and talking to her made him uncomfortable.

Why?

He glanced out the window, seeing nothing but white clouds. He knew exactly why Nikki got under his skin. She was smarter than he'd given her credit for. Her comment about competitive market research and branding told him that. And despite the chatter, she'd hit a nerve with her last question, bringing up a childhood Asher did his best not to think about. His default had been to cut her off.

She already put memories of his teen years at the forefront of his mind. He had no desire to go back even further. Concentrating on his iPad, he swiped and pulled up his Messenger App to talk with Derek.

Asher: *Any idea how long I'll be on this island?*

Derek: *You've only been in the air for an hour. Is she* *getting on your nerves already?*

Asher began replying, typing and deleting a few times, not wanting to insult Nikki or piss off his friend.

Derek: *She's talking a lot, isn't she?*

Asher expelled a breath that was half laugh, half groan of relief that his friend had nailed the problem before he'd had to spell it out.

Asher: *So much. Even more than my fourteen-year-old sister.*

Layla was actually his half sister, born to Michael and Serenity along with the seventeen-year-old triplets. Asher and his full siblings, Harrison, Zach, Nick, and Jade, were the products of Michael's marriage to their mother, Audrey, who had died by suicide after abandoning her family when Asher was nine.

His laptop dinged with Derek's reply, pulling him out of the unhappy past before he could dwell on it.

Asher glanced at the screen.

Derek: *Sorry, man. But I can't give you a time frame yet. Suck it up and make the best of it. She's a sweet girl if you give her a chance.*

Asher: *Will do.*

He tried to get back into the work he'd been doing before Nikki had interrupted him but couldn't concentrate, which left him with nothing to do but study the smart and beautiful woman who'd finally fallen asleep. Dark lashes fringed her pale skin, and her features were striking, emerald-green eyes hidden by her eyelids, and full and plush lips.

He shifted in his seat and those eyes suddenly opened, locking on his. Catching him staring. Her lips lifted in an adorable grin. He gritted his teeth and turned his gaze out the window.

The flight attendant came to offer them food and something to drink. Nikki asked for a glass of orange juice and Asher requested coffee. To his surprise, Nikki remained silent for the rest of the flight, and though he should be grateful, a part of him wished she'd ask him her silly questions. Because he liked that she wanted to get to know him?

He shrugged off the thought and suffered with the quiet until the pilot finally announced they'd be landing.

Nikki adjusted her seat belt and stared out the window as the plane began its descent.

Once on the ground, they walked down the steps and into the heat and humidity Asher was used to when on the island. Nikki's wide-eyed gaze took in their surroundings and came to rest on the white

Range Rover Asher kept at the house for airport pickups and errands.

Corey, his housekeeper's son and Asher's employee, waved as they stepped onto the tarmac.

"Who is that?" Nikki asked.

"He works for me. Runs the pool and the beach, manages the groundskeepers, etc. His mother, Maggie, is the housekeeper." She had worked for Michael and Serenity when Asher was young, helping his stepmother around the house when five kids, the triplets, and Layla became too much for one woman to handle alone. "Corey is picking us up."

The other man was in his mid-twenties and, like Asher, had a responsible streak. He worried about his single mother. Asher had needed an estate manager at the same time Serenity no longer needed full-time help around the house. The solution seemed obvious and Asher had offered Maggie the job here, and Corey had insisted on joining his mother. It had been a no-brainer for Asher to employ him as well.

Corey strode up to them with his usual smile. The man was perpetually happy and carefree, unlike Asher, whose siblings often ribbed him that he'd been born old and had never been a kid.

"Welcome back, Mr. Dare. Any luggage?" Corey asked.

"Hi, Corey. Yes, Ms. – Nikki has a suitcase and I

have my carry-on." He patted the bag hanging from his shoulder; work, his laptop, and tablet inside. Everything else he needed, from clothes to toiletries, was at the house.

"A pleasure to meet you, Nikki," Corey said.

"Same here."

He grinned at her, showing off dimples Asher only now noticed because Nikki stared at the man, a sweet expression on her face.

"Corey, luggage!" Asher snapped.

The other man rushed to grab her bag from where the pilot had unloaded her luggage, while Nikki frowned up at Asher. She wasn't happy with him, but at least she wasn't staring at his employee any longer.

"I noticed you didn't use my last name when introducing me to Corey," Nikki said. "Was that on purpose?"

He nodded. "I trust my people but better safe than sorry. Nobody needs to know who you are." Corey wouldn't sell her out, but no reason to give anyone the information if they didn't need it. And since Corey hadn't looked at Nikki with any familiarity, he obviously hadn't seen the photos.

"Good thinking," she murmured.

Corey rolled her suitcase to them. "Ready to go?"

Asher nodded.

Corey loaded the luggage in the back, then walked

around and opened both the front and back doors on the passenger side.

Asher offered Nikki the front seat but she shook her head. "I'm happy to sit in the back and take in the view," she said, climbing into the SUV.

"Suit yourself." Asher shut her door and took his seat in front.

Corey settled in and they were on their way. The house was only ten minutes from the small private airfield, and Asher had taken this ride endless times.

"It's beautiful here," Nikki said.

He glanced over his shoulder to see her staring out the window, sunglasses covering her eyes.

"It is," Corey agreed. "Wait until you're on the beach and view the ocean up close. It's like an endless stretch of sand, blue sky, and aqua water that makes you forget the rest of the world exists."

"Mmm. Can't wait." Nikki's expression softened even further as she considered his words and relaxed even more.

"Don't worry. I'll set your chair up in the best spot we have," Corey said.

Nikki's smile, despite all the trouble going on in her life, caused Asher's heart to beat faster, almost as if she'd kick-started the long-dormant organ in his chest.

"I'd appreciate that, Corey." Her voice was filled with gratitude to the other man, and Asher had had enough of their easy conversation.

She was *his* guest, dammit.

"Corey, update me on the issue with the pump in the pool," Asher said gruffly.

He caught Nikki frown again before he turned and faced forward, then listened to Corey's rundown of the status of things at the estate.

★ ★ ★

THE SUV PULLED up to a grand house with a white exterior and veranda that ran around the massive structure. Nikki immediately fell in love with the estate home, the palm trees and lush flora, all tropical visions she didn't see in New York or where she'd grown up in Washington, DC. Still annoyed with Asher for cutting off her conversation with Corey about nothing more than the beach and the view, she kept her opinion of the outside and landscaping of his home to herself. At least for now.

Without waiting for anyone to open her door, she pulled the handle herself. She stepped out of the SUV and back into heat and humidity that exceeded what they'd left behind in New York. After the air-conditioned vehicle, the heat of the sun felt good against her skin.

Closing her eyes, she tipped her head back and let

the warmth and vitamin D flood her system for a few brief seconds before refocusing on what was going on around her. Corey had just shut the back of the SUV and was walking up the stairs with her suitcase while Asher stood staring, his expression similar to when she'd awakened on the plane to find his gaze settled on her face.

He was such a contradiction, snapping at her and telling her to be quiet one minute, watching and studying her closely the next. Even with sunglasses covering his eyes, she felt the intensity of his gaze. What she couldn't decipher was what went on in his head. Though it went against her chatty and curious nature, she waited for him to talk first.

"Let's go in." He gestured for her to walk ahead of him, and she strode up the steps to the house, treading carefully in her heels. After today, she was ditching them for flip-flops.

He opened the door and placed a hand on her back as she stepped inside, causing a ripple of awareness to rush through her. Cool air greeted her, a combination of the air conditioner and large ceiling fans in the shape of palm leaves, turning over head. She blamed her hardening nipples on the AC and not Asher Dare's touch. Inside was pure Caribbean decor, dark wood, bamboo, light cream and baby-blue coloring.

"I love the design," she murmured, unable to keep her promise to herself not to compliment him.

"Thank you. My cousin Lucy is an interior designer. She's got great taste," Asher said, the smile telling her he liked both his house and his cousin.

And she liked how he looked. His white teeth flashed against tanned skin, and with the harsh lines gone, he was even more handsome than the grumbling alpha he usually presented.

"You should do that more often," she said, using his technique and staring at him.

"Do what?" he asked.

"Smile."

Before he could reply, a plump, attractive, older brunette rushed to greet them. "Asher, welcome home."

"Good to be here, Maggie." Asher embraced her and stepped back. "Maggie, this is my guest, Nikki." He turned. "Nikki, if you need anything, Maggie is the one who can help you."

"Nice to meet you, Maggie."

The other woman's smile was warm and welcoming. "Aren't you a pretty one?"

Nikki felt herself blush. "Thank you."

"It's good to see you bringing a *friend*," Maggie said to Asher, obviously knowing him well enough to be able to insinuate herself into his personal life.

Asher shook his head and shot Maggie a warning look she ignored, still smiling when she glanced back at Nikki.

"Give Nikki one of the rooms upstairs. I have work to do, so if you'll excuse me…" He walked away and strode across the open living area, his route taking him under an archway until he disappeared into a hallway or a room, Nikki had no idea which.

He'd left her alone with Maggie. So that was how it was going to be, she thought, trying not to be insulted. It was fine. She knew how to entertain herself.

"Well." Maggie spun to face her. "Let's get you settled, shall we? I'll give you a tour of the place, too." She pulled out her phone and sent a text. "Just letting Corey know which room to put your bags in."

Maggie gave her a quick tour of the house, which thankfully was an easy layout because Nikki was directionally impaired, to put it mildly. They walked through the state-of-the-art kitchen, where Nikki remembered to tell Maggie she was allergic to peanuts. One taste and she ended up covered in hives. It was odd, the allergy having developed after she turned eighteen, but the doctor told her one in five adults suffered with the issue.

Maggie was sweet, promised she'd be careful, and continued her tour. She showed Nikki the back exit to the veranda, which led to a patio with tables and chairs for outdoor eating, and gave her directions to the pool and the beach.

After escorting Nikki to her room, Maggie left her alone. She glanced out the window, took in the view, and decided to spend what remained of the day on the beach. Sometime during her tour, Corey had left her suitcase on a luggage stand at the foot of the queen-sized bed.

Nikki took out a bikini and changed into the bathing suit, pulling on a loosely crocheted cotton cover-up and flip-flops. She grabbed her beach bag and filled it with her phone, Airpods for music, and a few other things she might need, deciding she'd worry about unpacking later.

Then she headed downstairs, planning to ask Maggie where to find Corey so she could get towels and a lounge chair. As she neared the bottom step, he walked in the front door.

"Just the man I was looking for," she said, capturing his attention.

He stopped to wait for her, his gaze looking her over. "Hey. Headed for the beach or the pool?"

"I take it the bathing suit gave me away?" She laughed. "The beach. I was going to ask Maggie how to find you to hook me up with a lounge chair and towels."

He ran his fingers through his surfer-boy-styled

hair and grinned. "Happy to oblige. Come on and I'll get you set up."

"Great!"

She walked beside him through the house and out back, glad at least Maggie and Corey were pleasant to be around. Because her host obviously planned to be rude and distant for the duration of her stay.

★ ★ ★

IT DIDN'T TAKE long for Asher to set up his workstation in the room he used as his office whenever he was on the island. He had his twenty-four-inch screen and had brought his laptop along with him. Either would suffice. He changed into a pair of cargo shorts and a tee shirt and sat down behind the desk, pushing aside the fact that he'd abandoned Nikki as soon as he possibly could.

He tried to tell himself her chatter grated on his nerves, but the truth was the exact opposite. She was fun, easy to be around, and everyone liked her. Corey had been all too eager to offer his assistance on the beach, and Asher had almost bitten the guy's head off for flirting, when in reality, he had just been doing his job.

Then Maggie had been pleased to see him arrive with a woman, something Asher had never done before. Why? Mara, who'd come before Christy, had taught him if he opened up this part of his life to a female, she'd try to get her hooks into him and his money. He would never know if a woman liked him for himself or what he could buy her, and the sting of betrayal was too great to try again.

These days, he let women warm his bed, but they never insinuated themselves further. Which meant the only chitter-chatter he ever listened to were his sisters' and the kids in the family.

To keep Nikki at a necessary distance, he told himself she annoyed him. In reality, he could look at that gorgeous face all day and listen to her talk for hours. And considering her brother, Asher's friend, trusted him to take care of his sister? Keeping that distance was essential.

The sound of voices drifted through his open window that overlooked the ocean. He glanced out to see Nikki and Corey heading toward the beach, their laughter carrying back to Asher at his desk. Nikki wore a cover-up with more holes than fabric, a sight that had him clenching his fingers into fists.

He continued to watch the scene unfold. Corey left her and headed to the storage sheds where the lounge chairs and clean towels were kept and returned holding a chaise he set down then wrapped with towels.

And Nikki? She removed her cover-up. Beneath it,

she wore a hot-pink barely there bikini. Even from a distance, Asher's cock sprang to life. Though he could no longer hear them, the tinkling of Nikki's laughter rang in his ears. The view of her tiny bikini tortured him. Their joint enjoyment mocked him.

Even if he understood Corey was just being friendly while working, the guy was still closer to Nikki's age than Asher was. And he wasn't forbidden to touch her. *Yet.* Those would be the next words out of Asher's mouth… when he joined them by the water.

She hadn't been here for more than an hour and Asher was so fucked, he thought, as he stalked to his room so he could change for the beach.

★ ★ ★

NIKKI TOOK OUT the sunscreen she'd packed and lathered up all the parts of her body she could reach. Courtesy of her mother's Italian family, she was lucky enough to have olive skin that didn't burn, but she still had to worry about things like wrinkles and skin cancer. Once she was finished rubbing in the lotion, she slipped on her sunglasses, leaned back in the comfortable chaise, and closed her eyes.

Instead of putting in earbuds and listening to music, she tried to let the rush of the ocean relax her. But with nothing to distract her, the swirling humiliation of her life came rushing back. She imagined her parents were meeting with their PR people and losing their minds, not that she'd heard from them since Derek had told her mother off earlier.

She ignored the pit in her stomach that formed whenever they disappointed her… usually as a result of her disappointing them first, she thought and let out a long sigh.

"What's on your mind?" a familiar but surprising voice asked.

She opened her eyes to find Asher standing over her. "I thought you had work to do?"

"I couldn't concentrate." Thanks to the aviators covering his eyes, she couldn't read his expression. Then again, even when she could see his whole face, the man's moods and feelings were tough to decipher.

He lowered himself to the edge of her lounger and sat, forcing her to pull her feet back to make room—instead of asking Corey to get him his own lounge. See, she mused. Confusing.

"You didn't answer. What's on your mind that had you sighing so loudly?" He shifted, knees toward her, so they could talk face-to-face.

"A lot has happened since I woke up this morning. I'm just trying to process it all." She and Asher weren't close enough for her to open up to him about always falling short in her parents' eyes. "And you didn't answer *me*. I thought you had to work?"

He ran his hand over that sexy beard before finally replying. "I wanted to make sure you were okay."

That was surprisingly… sweet. "Thank you. It's been a rough day."

He nodded. "I'm sure it has. Want to talk about it?" he asked, showing her yet another side of Asher Dare.

She considered it for point-two seconds and shook her head.

She already had the impression he didn't think highly of her. She'd be better off not going into detail about the photos and her fear of someone watching her in her apartment. All her honesty would do was make him think worse of her than he already did. It seemed to be a running theme. Her parents, the girls on the modeling circuit, now Asher. Thank God for her brother, who believed the best about her and defended her no matter what circumstances she found herself in.

She glanced at the blue water and lapping waves. "I think I'll take a walk. Get my feet wet."

She was about to stand when he grasped her ankle, his warm, strong grip taking her by surprise. "Sunscreen?"

"Already done." Again, she found it nice that he'd ask.

"Even your back? Because it's easy to burn when you're in the water."

Her lips twitched as she tried not to grin. He was *so* not going to like her answer. "I can't reach my back," she said, eyeing him as she tried hard not to let her smile and laughter escape.

With a put-out groan, he extended a hand, palm up, a silent, grudging offer to help.

She studied him with shameless curiosity. "Asher Dare, are you trying to get your hands on me?" She couldn't deny the possibility had her body buzzing in the most incredible ways.

He shook his head, gripping the back of his neck. "Just hand over the lotion," he muttered.

Now grinning, she did just that.

Then, grabbing her hair, she pulled it into a messy bun so it wouldn't get dirty and tipped her head down, giving him easy access. From the corner of her eye, she saw him pour the cream on his palm, and soon he was massaging the lotion into her back.

She wasn't sure what felt better, the cool cream or his big, strong hands kneading her skin, but one thing she knew, she liked him touching her.

A lot.

★ ★ ★

By the time Asher finished massaging sunscreen into Nikki's soft flesh, his cock was just the opposite. Rock hard and erect. Unaware, she slid her legs off the other side of the lounge and rose to her feet. Her bikini bottoms had slipped up, revealing her ass cheeks, and he swallowed a loud groan.

"Want to join me?" She glanced at him over her shoulder.

He shook his head. "Maybe in a few minutes." When he could stand without his erection being visible.

She shrugged. "Suit yourself," she said and strode off toward the water.

With no one around, he adjusted himself and deliberately did not watch her little strut because that would only be more torture. He was already doing things that went against the promises he'd made to keep a safe distance from the temptress. And the joke was, he still didn't believe she was deliberately being provocative. She was just… Nikki.

He didn't know her well, but she was more than his preconceived notions based on another woman from another time in his life. Even his stubborn, arrogant ass could admit that.

"Come on, join me!" Nikki called, waving an arm to get his attention as she drifted toward deeper waters.

More at ease now that his attention had drifted off her soft skin and ripe curves, but uncomfortable with how far out she was floating, he rose. Pulling off his shirt and tossing it on the chair, he strode down to the ocean, wading in to get close to Nikki.

"It's warm!" Her head bobbed above the water, but he was relieved to realize her feet were still on the floor, letting him relax.

He drifted closer and she splashed him, the flying droplets hitting him in the face. He sputtered and rubbed his eyes to relieve the sting of the salt.

"Oops!" Her green eyes twinkled as she laughed.

He shook his head and surprised himself by splashing her back. A water fight ensued and even his head ended up soaking wet. He ducked under and came up laughing, shocking the shit out of him. When was the last time he'd *played*, let alone had fun? Even his recent trip to Vegas with the guys had been more about watching than actually indulging in anything more than a drink or two.

He glanced at the cause of his un-Asher-like behavior. Nikki stood in the water, catching her breath, a big smile on her face. Her hair was slicked back, making her green eyes even more prominent against her olive skin.

God, she was gorgeous. Against his better judgment, and contrary to his plans and the promises he'd made, his cock once again reminded him he desired this free-spirited girl. And that was the thought that stopped him. Not just his promise to her brother, though that was a huge consideration, but she was too damned young. Talk about a scandal waiting to happen.

But dammit, she made him feel young and alive. Not that thirty-three was old, for Christ's sake, but he still had twelve years on her.

"That was fun." She took a few steps back and bobbed in the water.

He ran his hand through his hair and nodded. "Yeah, it was," he said, unwilling to burst her happy bubble. She had too much worry on her shoulders and deserved to forget her troubles. But it was time for him to rebuild some walls.

"I'm going to go back–" He was cut off by the sound of Nikki's scream and he rushed up to her. "What's wrong?"

She looked at him with wide eyes, frantically waving her hands. "I think I was stung on my leg. I want to feel for it but I'm scared what I'll find."

"Don't touch," he instructed. "It's probably from a jellyfish." And if so, there was every chance she still had tentacles in her leg. Not that he'd tell her that yet.

Her eyes opened wide. "Please don't say you have to pee on me," she muttered.

He felt his lips lift. "No. That's an old wives' tale. Come on." He bent down, picked her up, and carried her out of the water. "I'm going to bring you inside. We'll take a look at it then."

She wrapped her arms around his neck and rested her head against his chest. Trusting him. He wondered how she'd feel knowing he found her soft sighs and curvy body, cold from the water and trembling against his chest, too damned arousing.

He began the walk back to the house when Corey came rushing toward them. "What's wrong?" the other man asked.

"Nikki was stung by a jellyfish."

At Asher's words, her grip around his neck tightened.

"I'll go grab the first-aid kit from the shed," Corey said.

"No. I'll take her inside." Although first aid was part of Corey's job, Asher didn't want the other man's hands anywhere near Nikki's skin.

Corey lifted both arms, palms out, in a sign of hands-off. He obviously got the message.

Knowing that the pain of a sting could be excruciating, Asher made a beeline for his bathroom, where he had a kit beneath the vanity.

Chapter Four

ASHER DIDN'T PAUSE until he reached the bathroom. He lowered Nikki to her feet, pulled a decorative stool from the corner and settled her on it. "Let me see."

She raised her leg. Large red welts marred her flesh, and it looked like there were tentacles still embedded in the skin.

He winced but didn't say a word. He opened the door to the vanity and pulled out his first-aid kit, which included tweezers for just this purpose, along with a bottle of alcohol and one of vinegar, also kept here for this kind of emergency.

"You're prepared."

"You have to be around here. Stings are fairly common."

He unscrewed the top of the alcohol bottle and ran some over the tweezers to sterilize them before coming back to her. "Let's move the chair closer to the tub so your leg hangs into it. I want to run vinegar over the stingers before I pull them out."

She grimaced but did as he asked, draping her leg over the ledge. He soaked her skin in the vinegar, doing his best to focus on her injury and not her coconut-scented smell, delicious despite the horrible stench of the vinegar. Not to mention the amount of bare flesh revealed thanks to the skimpy, wet bikini she wore.

Once he finished, she rose and he pulled the chair closer to the toilet. He sat on the seat cover and patted his thighs.

She lowered herself onto the stool and stretched her leg across his lap. He picked up the tweezer, meeting her gaze before he got to work. Her fear was palpable, and he was determined to do this fast.

"Ready?" he asked.

She bit down on her lower lip and nodded.

Pulling out the stingers wasn't fun. He felt her stiffen, noted the tightening of her muscles and the occasional sniffle. But he managed to finish. "All done. And you should know, you're braver than Harrison. He cried like a baby."

She laughed as he'd intended, the sound hitting him in the chest in an unfamiliar way.

"Thank you," she murmured and slid her leg off his thighs, and he felt the loss of her body heat.

"Are you okay?" he asked.

She nodded. "Yeah. It hurts but I know it'll pass."

He rose and put everything on the counter back into the cabinet before handing her a tube of cortisone cream. "Why don't you shower, let the warm water rinse over your leg, and put this on after? I'll leave some Benadryl and ibuprofen in your room for you to take, too."

"Asher?"

He turned just as she stepped up to him, way too close for comfort, her tanned skin glowing and that exotic coconut scent that was beyond arousing wrapping around him. She looked up, those eyes liquid pools of green pulling him in.

"I just wanted to say thank you. I know you didn't want to bring me here and now I've already been trouble–"

He couldn't tear his gaze from her lips, lush and wet from the swipe of her tongue. One second he was staring and the next he'd dipped his head and covered her mouth with his. At the first touch of his lips, she stilled, her surprise evident, but she immediately wrapped her arms around his neck and kissed him back.

With her on board, he swept his tongue inside. He tasted her, salty from the ocean with a hint of sweetness that was all Nikki. The woman he'd been keeping at a distance when he wanted nothing more than to lose himself inside her.

She was everything he wasn't. Fun, sweet, happy, young. His friend's sister. The friend who trusted him.

And as she rubbed herself against his hard erection, her tight nipples grazing his chest, he knew he had to stop before things went any further.

He raised his head. With the counter behind him, he couldn't step back, but he'd ended the kiss and made his point.

She moaned at the loss of his mouth and did what he couldn't. Moved away and put distance between them. But her eyes were glazed with need, and she had a dreamy expression on her face only a young woman could manage.

"Don't look at me like that," he said in a gruff voice.

She breathed heavily, her breasts rising and falling, her cleavage beckoning for him to lick. And there was that tiny bathing suit he'd be jerking off to tonight.

He needed to adjust his cock but refrained. "This can't happen again." He had to say it out loud. For his own sake as well as for hers.

His words cleared the lust-filled fog from her eyes and she widened her gaze. "I see. Okay, then. Umm, I'll just be going now." Cheeks flushed red in embarrassment, she grabbed the cortisone and fled, giving him a perfect view of her ass cheeks peeking out from the sides of her bathing suit bottoms.

"Son of a bitch." He pressed his palms against his eyes and groaned.

He shook his head hard in an attempt to clear the remaining need Nikki inspired. Then he shut the bathroom door and stripped before stepping under the waterfall showerhead. But not even turning the temperature to cold alleviated the raging desire.

He soaped up his hand and grabbed his cock. Bracing one hand on the wall, he began to glide his palm up and down his straining shaft. He closed his eyes and an image of Nikki appeared, her skin glistening in the sun, her smile wide as she knelt before him. As he imagined her sucking him into her warm mouth, he tightened his grip and groaned.

In his mind, *she* licked him, circling the head, teasing his shaft, and doing a damned fine job of bringing him close. Her hands cupped his balls that had drawn up tight, and before he knew it, his orgasm flashed through him. He came hard, spurting over the shower walls and floor, the release easing some of the tension that had been riding him.

But it wasn't enough. Nothing short of burying himself inside her would slake his need. And that couldn't happen. No matter how much he desired it.

He stepped out of the shower and dried off, stalking into the bedroom, where he dressed in a pair of shorts and a tee shirt.

He called to Maggie to bring Nikki medicine for the sting. Then he killed time on his laptop, answering emails and catching up with a few things before his stomach growled, letting him know it was time for dinner.

He assumed he'd meet up with Nikki, and with a little luck, they could ignore the kiss and move forward without having to discuss it.

He walked into the dining area, where Maggie stood fussing over a table with one place setting. "Asher! Are you hungry?"

He nodded. "I am. What do we have tonight?"

"The chef made your favorite, apricot chicken. Do you want to eat in here or outside?"

He glanced out the windows to the empty table on the veranda. "You're already set up here. Inside is fine." He took in the one setting again. "Isn't Nikki joining us?"

She shook her head. "The poor girl wasn't feeling well. Her leg was a little swollen, so I gave her some Benadryl and a painkiller and brought her meal to her room. She was going to eat and turn in early."

He ran his hand through his hair. "Are you certain she didn't need a doctor?"

Maggie shook her head. "No. I think she'll feel better in the morning."

He hoped so. Because he should have checked on her instead of giving in to the urge to bury himself in business and put her out of his mind. It wasn't like it had worked, and now she probably thought he was an asshole.

Which, after his reaction to their kiss, he really was.

★ ★ ★

NIKKI WOKE UP, surprised she'd slept. She rarely got a good night's sleep, which was what made the fact that someone managed to take photos and catch her unaware, all the more shocking. Shaking off those thoughts, she focused on last night. Between the pain from the sting and the hurt from Asher's response to their kiss, she'd assumed she would have tossed and turned. But the Benadryl had made her tired, so maybe combined with the entire day's stress, it had knocked her out.

Better than having Asher's voice repeating over and over in her head. *This can't happen again.* In other words, it'd taken him point-two seconds to regret it. Actually, his regret had come mid-lip-lock, never mind she'd felt his thick erection pressing against her stomach, leaving her wanting. Ugh.

She checked out her leg. The sting area was less swollen, though she could definitely see where the jellyfish had done its job. She drank the smoothie Maggie had left outside her door, popped some ibuprofen, and decided not to brave the beach again.

Instead, she'd go into town and do some shopping, maybe find a café on the water where she could have lunch. Later, she'd call her brother so he wouldn't worry about her.

With a little luck, she'd get out of the house before Asher came downstairs and avoid his broodiness and mood swings. She was certain that given her issues with direction, she'd get lost, but she'd just take Corey's phone number so she could call him when she wanted to go home. He'd find her and bring her back.

She grabbed her bag and sunglasses and walked down the stairs, luckily bumping into him coming out of the kitchen. He looked casual in his checkered long shorts and white tee shirt.

"Hey!" He strode up to her, his concerned gaze meeting hers. "Are you okay?" He glanced down at her leg and winced. "Looks painful."

The red welts weren't attractive but she could handle the discomfort. "Actually, this is much better than it was last night. I took some over-the-counter painkillers, and I plan to go on with my day. What are the chances you could drive me into town?"

He hesitated and she immediately understood. "You're afraid Asher will be angry."

"Well, under normal circumstances, I wouldn't care and take you anyway but…"

"I get it. But because driving is your job, shouldn't

you be able to do it without worrying?" She tipped her head to one side, thoroughly certain of her logic.

He shook his head and grinned. "You have a valid point. Looks like I'm driving you." He extended his bent arm for her to take, and she went to hook her arm through his when she heard footsteps pounding down the stairs.

"What's going on?" Asher asked as he reached the bottom.

"I asked Corey to take me to town. After all, isn't he your driver?" Nikki challenged him first. She wasn't about to let Asher use his position as owner of the estate to give Corey a hard time over something she wanted.

Asher frowned. "I was going to head there myself. I'll take you. Corey, you're needed at the garage." He didn't bark the order at the other man, and Nikki knew he was modulating his tone so she wouldn't get mad at him.

Little did he realize she was already annoyed. No way was he already planning to go into town. He just didn't want Corey to be the one to take her. He was jealous. After walking out on her last night and not checking on her at all, he was back to mixed messages.

Well, Mr. Dare needed to learn that some people might bow to his orders, but she'd stood up to stronger men than him. If Nikki could handle the imposing

Senator Bettencourt and his demanding wife, her *parents*, she could definitely deal with Asher's mercurial ass.

★ ★ ★

THE MOMENT ASHER walked down the stairs, he caught sight of Nikki in a flirty short skirt, cropped top, and flip-flops, her hair pulled into a messy bun, talking to Corey. She was planning a trip to town, and his gut twisted into an uncomfortable knot.

The island was relatively safe but he'd feel better if she wasn't alone. And he didn't want her spending her time with Corey. Fuck. Jealousy was not Asher's normal M.O. but there it was.

Did he want to take the day and go shopping? No, yet before he knew it, the words were out of his mouth, and they were in the Rover, on their way. He took the bridge to Eleuthera, expecting Nikki to ask questions and point out the beauty surrounding them, but Miss Usually Chatty had been silent the entire thirty-minute trip.

Asher had no doubt she was pissed at him and he didn't blame her, but it wasn't in his nature to apologize. Saying *I'm sorry* wouldn't put him at an advantage in business. But Nikki wasn't business.

"I'm not used to seeing people drive on the left

side of the road," she said, surprising him by initiating conversation.

"You adjust but it's not easy at first." They drove past the small shops and through narrow streets until Asher saw an open parking spot.

He pulled in, put the car in park, and cut the engine. Turning to face her, he slid an arm over the passenger side of the car.

"How are you feeling?" He hoped to break the earlier tension before they spent a long day together.

"My leg itches and still stings. Hurts some. But I'll manage." Her expression didn't change and her shoulders were pulled back straight.

From what Derek had told him about the Bettencourts and their frustration with their daughter, Asher had a feeling Nikki always had to deal with things on her own. Her resilience pointed to a person who knew how to take care of herself, and she wasn't giving in to Asher. And he normally could get most people to back down. Unless they were part of his family, then all bets were off.

Since Derek had sent her here to escape judgment and stress, Asher shouldn't be adding to her problems or making her uncomfortable.

He cleared his throat. "I'm sorry. I should have checked on you last night." The words weren't easy, and from her widened eyes, she hadn't expected the apology.

"Thank you."

She studied him until he felt uncomfortable in his own skin, and Asher was never that.

"Something tells me that wasn't easy for you," she said, tipping her head to the side as she studied him.

If she only knew.

She unhooked her seat belt, and he blew out a breath, relieved she was moving on.

"Ready to go?" he asked.

She nodded. "I was hoping Corey would point out places to souvenir shop, and I wanted to have lunch at a small café. So I hope you're ready to play tour guide."

He shook his head at what he'd gotten himself into. "I'll do my best."

She smiled at him, all earlier tension gone. With her makeup-free face, she was more beautiful than any woman he'd had on his arm at the varied fundraisers and galas he'd attended. Women with full glam makeup and sexy dresses didn't come close to Nikki.

Man, he was fucked.

"Let's go." He climbed out of the vehicle and came around to meet her.

She hooked her arm in his and they went shopping.

Nikki spent over an hour in various souvenir

shops, where she bought herself beaded necklaces and bracelets, including a set for Maggie, which stumped Asher. When he'd asked, she'd informed him that the older woman had been kind to her, checking her leg and making sure she had round-the-clock Benadryl and ibuprofen.

Which was more than her own mother had ever done, a statement that stayed with him. Even if Asher's mom hadn't been present mentally and later physically, he'd always had Serenity. Who he'd never appreciated as much as he now realized he should have.

"Ooh look!" Nikki held up a long tie-dye dress against herself. "Yep. I'll take it!"

She purchased that item along with other dresses and resort wear without trying things on. He assumed as a model, she had an eye for what fit her. At their next stop, a gallery, she bought an original painting of the pink sand both Eleuthera and Harbour Island were known for, exclaiming how it would go perfectly in her room in New York.

As soon as she'd said the words *her room*, the excitement in her eyes had dimmed. She'd muttered something about the damn pictures taken there and she'd shut down, her happiness gone.

He was determined to get it back and see her smile.

Asher loaded her purchases into the SUV, and they walked to the café he had in mind for lunch. "So this place is relaxing. It's owned by a husband and wife who grew up on the island," he said as they strode up three wooden plank steps surrounded by palm trees. "Don't expect a quick meal. We'll probably be here for a couple of hours."

Which made him wonder why he'd chosen this restaurant. Didn't he have work to do? As opposed to watching her eyes light up like the color of the ocean when it turned more green than blue.

"Sounds perfect!" Nikki practically bounced with happiness as he'd hoped.

He admired her ability to put the shit in her life out of her head and enjoy the here and now. He didn't know many people with that ability. Hell, he always had fifty thousand things going on in his mind and was aggravated with about half of them.

Yet the last hour or so, walking around town, listening to Nikki ask the shopkeepers questions about their items for sale, watching her expressive face as she learned more about the island and its people? He hadn't thought about anything other than her.

He pulled open the door to the restaurant and let her walk in ahead of him. They were greeted by a pretty young woman with glowing brown skin and braids that fell to her waist. Asher recognized her as the owners' daughter.

"Hello, Mr. Dare. It's so good to see you back," she said with a welcoming smile.

"I've told you, it's Asher. You're home from school. You graduated?" he asked.

She nodded with a proud tilt to her chin.

Asher turned to Nikki. "Nikki, this is Aayla. Aayla went to culinary school in the States." He gestured back and forth between the women. "And Aayla, this is my… friend Nikki." He stumbled over what to call Nikki.

But she grinned at the woman who wasn't more than a couple of years older than her. "It's nice to meet you." Nikki took a step closer. "I love your necklace." A small clock face sat on a gold chain.

"Thanks! I bought it when I was in New York," Aayla said.

"And I bought things in some gift shops here to wear at home."

The women chatted some more until Aayla picked up paper menus. "Come. It's still quiet. There's a spot out back overlooking the water." She led them outside to a table for four.

Asher gestured for Nikki to take a chair facing the shoreline, and she delicately sat down, making sure her short skirt covered her ass. Jesus.

He'd planned to take the chair across from her until Aayla placed the second menu on the spot beside Nikki. "So you both have an ocean view," she said. "Can I get you drinks?"

"I'll have a virgin piña colada, please," Nikki said.

The nonalcoholic choice took him by surprise.

"Mr. Dare?" Aayla asked.

He glanced at the drink menu in a Lucite holder. "When in… the Bahamas," he mused. "I'll have a Long Island coquito."

"Great. Do you want to look at the menu and order or I can have my father surprise you?"

Nikki glanced at him. "I'm good with surprises as long as it doesn't have peanuts. I'm allergic," she explained.

Another tidbit he now knew about her, including how much she enjoyed living.

"Surprising us sounds good to me, too," Asher said.

Aayla nodded. "I'll be back."

Left alone, Nikki immediately turned toward him. "What's in your drink?" she asked, her chatty curiosity showing through.

He glanced at the plastic holder for confirmation. "Gin, tequila, coconut rum, and coconut vodka."

So he could imagine he was tasting Nikki as he drank, while smelling the coconut-scented lotion she'd obviously rubbed into her skin this morning.

"Mmm. That sounds delicious." Her voice sounded unusually husky, and his cock stiffened in response.

Since he couldn't do anything to draw attention to the issue in his lap, he opened the napkin and covered himself.

Nikki did the same, her reasons having more to do with good manners.

"Why aren't you having a real drink?" he asked.

"I'm still taking Benadryl. I'm managing fine and don't want to risk getting sleepy."

He nodded. "Makes sense."

His phone buzzed and he pulled it from his pocket, glanced at the screen, noting it was a business associate who could wait. He tapped the ignore button and put the phone facedown on the table.

Which made him realize Nikki hadn't looked at her cell the entire time they'd been in town. Even the triplets, guys not girls, couldn't stay off their phones. On the plane, Nikki had mentioned wanting to avoid social media. Maybe that was still the case.

"Is everything okay at home?" he asked, knowing that was the easiest segue into the conversation.

She lifted her shoulders in a slight shrug. "I'll in check with Derek this afternoon."

He wondered about friends and recalled Derek saying she didn't trust people easily. He studied her profile as she looked over the ocean, a sudden quiet and sadness overtaking her, so unlike the bouncy, excited woman of this morning.

She must be lonely and her life emptier than he'd realized. "Do you want to talk about what happened to you?" he heard himself ask, taken off guard by his own words.

She turned to him. "I think it would help. You know, to get things off my chest. Or out of my head, really."

He gave her his full attention, resting an elbow on the table and meeting her gaze. "Let's have it, then."

She sighed and was about to talk when Aayla silently put their drinks on the table and, as if sensing they were in a private conversation, stepped away.

Nikki took a sip of her frozen drink, her lips pursing around the straw. He closed his eyes for a brief second so he wouldn't stare at that mouth and took a large swig of his beverage.

"I'm not even sure what happened or how," she said. "I woke up the other morning to an influx of notifications and calls. I clicked on a link my agent sent me, and suddenly I was staring at nude pictures of me sleeping *in my own bedroom*." Her cheeks flushed and she grabbed for her glass again, almost gulping, then she winced. "Ouch. Brain freeze." She rubbed at her temple and groaned.

He waited until her facial expression told him the

sensation passed. "Better?"

She nodded. "The fact that someone took the photos in my personal space is scary as hell. And before you ask, no. No boyfriends, no men, no one staying over in more than six months. No girlfriends, either."

He refused to delve into why he liked that no men had been at her place in a long time. "Could the pictures be photoshopped?" he asked.

She shook her head. "I sleep nude."

Well, that was a truth and a visual he might never get out of his head. "Shit."

"That about sums it up. I don't know why these things keep happening to me that end up in the press, creating scandals and embarrassing my parents."

"Like the drugs at the airport?" he asked, deciding to go all in with this conversation.

How else could he get to know her better? To help her somehow? If Asher was nothing else, he was the protector in his family, the oldest of the original siblings he'd looked out for all their lives.

She nodded. "Like that. I don't know how my father suppressed that story but he managed. I swear to you, I don't do drugs. I didn't have them on me. I didn't put them in my suitcase."

"I believe you." At one time he hadn't been sure. But this woman who wouldn't drink if she was on Benadryl hadn't been nor was she now using drugs.

He'd underestimated her. Again.

"Thank you," she said on a sigh of relief. She wrapped her hands around the rounded bottom of her glass. "And while I'm at it, I owe you an apology for my behavior that day. I was scared. They kept me in a hot room with no air conditioning. My parents, when I finally reached them, were screaming at me. Mostly my mother was." She gestured as she spoke, getting worked up as she told the story.

"Stop." He grasped her hand, aware of the size difference, his large fingers over her smaller ones, and how cold her palm was from the frozen drink. He wrapped his fingers around hers. "You don't owe me an apology. I get it."

She met his gaze and a wry smile pursed her lips. "Maybe *now* you do. But back then? You thought I was a spoiled kid, right?"

His face grew warm and why was that? Since when did he get embarrassed? "I might have believed that, yes." Thanks to his dealings with his model ex-girlfriend, youth, and a stubborn need to think he was right. "But I know better now. What else has happened? You mentioned *these things keep* happening to you."

She sighed. "Well, my contract makes me sound like I'm difficult." She pulled her hand back and rested her elbows on the table, her chin on her hands.

"In what way?"

"I can't eat peanuts, so that has to be spelled out so there are none in food supplied to everyone at a shoot or on a runway walk. Otherwise, I need my own specially made meal provided for me." She used her straw to mix the contents of the thick drink and took a sip.

He did the same with his. "Sounds reasonable."

"It is. But told without context, it can be misconstrued, and someone leaked the contents of my contract, making me sound like a demanding diva." She wrinkled her nose in disgust. "The next day, at a high-end photo shoot, the other girls whispered behind my back, treating me like I was too difficult to be around."

Jesus. No wonder Derek said she had problems making and trusting friends.

"And that was only part of it. Social media sites posted exaggerated stories," she went on. "Girls I work with claimed I would only drink a certain kind of expensive water, that someone had to pick almonds out of my salad, rude things like that." She shrugged, as if she were used to it.

But how did anyone get used to people spewing lies and being mean around them?

"I tried to let it go, but my mother hates my name out there in any negative way, and she gave me hell about my behavior. As if she wasn't fully aware of what was in the contract and why."

"Why wouldn't your parents take your side? Be there for you?" Asher's family would go to bat for any one of them.

She swallowed hard. "Because all that matters to her is that nothing reflects negatively on my father. His goal has always been the White House. Nothing could get in the way. Not even their kids."

He shook his head, unable to comprehend it but believing her entirely. Derek had always said as much, but he was the prodigal son, the good guy who never got into trouble. Apparently that role fell to Nikki.

"That all sucks," he muttered. "I take it there's more?" He wanted her to purge it all.

She nodded, staring at him with those trusting green eyes. He now understood how precious that trust was.

Reaching over, he squeezed her hand, urging her to continue.

"I get lost easily," she said.

"Okay?" he asked, unsure what the issue was. "I assume many people are geographically challenged."

She sighed. "I have a form of directional dyslexia, though that's not the preferred term."

He wrinkled his brows, still confused.

She tucked a strand of hair that had fallen out of

her bun behind her ear. "It's complicated but I truly have no sense of direction. I have to reteach myself left and right and I often forget. I can't read a map. My parents never believed it was real, but trust me, it is." She went back to circling the straw in her glass.

"And this impacts your career," he assumed.

"Yes. But I'm aware of the potential for being late, so I'd leave early wherever I was staying. Even if I take a car and give them the address, finding where I'm going once I step out of the vehicle is a challenge. Add in a foreign country and language and it's always worse."

"That can't be easy."

"It's not. I was late to photo shoots and that looks bad. It adds to the things that *make Nikki difficult*," she said with finger quotes around the words. "It gave the girls reasons to be annoyed with me. Forget the fact that many of them went from the hotel to a shoot together and nobody called me to go with them."

"They were jealous," he concluded. "Of your family name and your beauty. No doubt they worried you'd outshine them."

She blushed but didn't deny the possibility. "Anyway, you get the gist. I don't like sounding sorry for myself."

"And you don't. You sound like someone with legitimate issues who hasn't been treated fairly. And now with the photos taken without your permission, you're at your breaking point."

She tipped her head to the side. "How are you so understanding and aware?"

He laughed. "I'm the oldest with four younger full siblings and another four half siblings, but that's my story."

"For another day?" she asked hopefully, making him squirm in his seat.

Instead of replying, he kept the focus on her. "What I suggest is that you take advantage of being on the island. Leave your troubles in New York for now. They'll be there when you get home."

Not only because she needed the break but he missed seeing her bright smile and the light that was usually around her when she was happy.

Before she could answer, Aayla returned with plates of appetizers and placed them on the table, explaining the type of sauces on the fresh shrimp and crabs. "We had a very large party come in, so my father is busy. He says hello and he'll try to come out of the kitchen before you leave."

"Thank you," Asher said. "Send him my best."

The young woman smiled, nodded, and headed back inside.

Asher served them both, putting the food on his and Nikki's plates, causing the delicious smells to assault his senses.

"Wow. This looks amazing," she said, picking up her fork and knife, cutting into the food. She took a bite and moaned.

The sound went straight to his cock, desire for this complicated woman settling inside him. Something that didn't change throughout the long meal while he learned more about her past and the woman she'd become. Discovering how wrong he'd been about her only added to his need. He *liked* the woman she was. Despite the age difference, she was more mature than most of the women he'd dated.

More than once he'd caught himself staring at Nikki's mouth, wanting to taste those lips again. By the time he paid the check and they were in the SUV headed to his estate, Asher wanted nothing more than to pick her up, carry her to his room, and bury himself deep inside her.

Scarier still was the need to take care of her, to make the emotional pain and loneliness she experienced go away. And what would her brother and his close friend think of that?

Chapter Five

LATER THAT EVENING, Nikki stretched her legs out on the bed in her room. She was still stuffed from the huge meal she'd eaten today. As Asher had predicted, they'd sat for a couple of hours, sharing appetizers, the main course, and dessert. He'd kept the focus of conversation on her, asking how she'd gotten into modeling and learning more about her. Given his interest, she'd opened up.

About how, as a child, while her father was settled in DC, building his career, her mother had tried to mold Nikki into the perfect show pony. She'd been sent to private schools, enrolled in pageants, and forced to smile for photos and talk to adults more than she'd ever been with other kids. It was no wonder she'd never made close friends. For her mother, Nikki modeling was a natural progression.

For Nikki, it was too similar to pageantry. She'd wanted to be *herself*, not her mother's protégé. But even as a teenager, she'd realized that, if she wanted to get out from under their thumbs, she needed money. At fifteen, she began to model.

When the career demanded she travel, she was

homeschooled with tutors and over the years, earned her GED. Around the same time, her father needed his wife around him for political appearances and Nikki got used to being on her own.

Finally, at eighteen, her parents had allowed her to move to New York where Derek lived, not to LA, which had been her first choice. She'd wanted to get as far away from them as possible but she loved her brother and he'd been happy to have her nearby.

Asher had been understanding about her past, and she'd seen a different side to him today. Watching him talk to Aayla and her father with interest and respect, then his listening to Nikki, he'd been so different than the uptight, aloof man she'd originally met.

The persona he'd unfortunately returned to as soon as they'd walked back into the house. He'd curtly informed her he was going to his office to work. It was almost as if he wanted to distance himself from the warmer man he'd let escape today.

Nikki wondered what his background was and what pain he hid from the world. Though she wouldn't pry, she hoped to get close enough to find out.

Her cell rang, and since she'd spoken to Derek before hooking the phone up to charge, she doubted the caller was her brother. She grabbed the cell from the nightstand and saw Winter, her neighbor's name, flashing on the screen.

Surprised, Nikki answered. "Hello?"

"Hi, Nikki. I'm calling to see how you're doing," Winter said in that warm tone Nikki automatically responded to.

"I'm okay. I'm staying—"

"No. Don't tell me where you are." Winter's words were a surprise. "I stopped by your apartment a few times and nobody answered, so I figured you'd left town."

Nikki didn't reply. She'd only planned to say she was staying *with a friend* because she wasn't sure she could trust Winter… or anyone.

"I want to be someone you can talk to," Winter said into the silence. "And if you tell me where you are and it gets out, you'll never know."

Nikki blew out a long breath. "Thank you for that." She had such a deep longing for the kind of friendship Winter offered, just the sound of the other woman's voice triggered hope they could one day be true friends. "I'm okay. Staying off social media helps, and I'm trying not to think about what happened."

"I'm glad. The reporters cleared out from the street out front, if it helps to know that," Winter said.

"It does, actually." Though she hoped they hadn't swarmed her parents instead. That was a hassle she didn't need. "I appreciate you checking in on me,"

Nikki said.

"And I'll do it again. Take care, okay?"

Nikki swallowed over the lump in her throat. "I will. Thanks." She disconnected and laid the phone down on the nightstand.

Tired, she glanced out the window. It had begun to rain, and she closed her eyes, listening to the soft taps against the house. Next thing she knew, she was startled awake by a clap of thunder and jumped up in bed. That noise had always scared her, and eventually sent her running into Derek's room where she'd make herself comfortable on the floor.

As an adult, a lingering fear of storms remained but as she was alone on this island, she had to suck it up. Just as she did at home. She rose from the bed and pulled a sleep shirt from one of the drawers, then walked to the bathroom, where she washed up, brushed her teeth, and got ready for bed, this time for the night.

Back in the bedroom, she glanced at a digital clock. Eleven p.m. She'd somehow managed to doze for a long time and was worried she wouldn't fall back to sleep. Which meant she'd be in for a long night.

Lightning flashed in the window, followed by a crack of thunder that had her jumping at the sudden sound. Shit. She climbed back into her bed and picked up her phone, opening a book she'd been reading and trying hard to get into the story.

When that didn't distract her, she even googled things to do on the island. But the wind picked up, slamming the rain against the house, and her heart beat harder against her chest. God, why couldn't she get over this stupid phobia? Nothing was going to happen to her. She was safe inside. She reiterated the words over and over but couldn't calm down.

She'd packed so quickly, she'd left her soundproof headphones at home, and since those didn't completely block out the noise of a storm, the ones she had with her, the small ones that went into her ears, wouldn't work, either.

With a sigh, she closed her eyes and rested her head on the pillow, trying to regulate her breathing. Another flash of lightning and immediate thunder broke her attempted in-and-out rhythm. The light and noise came more often now, almost on top of each other, and the windswept rain pelted the house even harder. They must be in the center of the storm.

She sat upright in bed, her fingers in a death grip around the comforter, wishing she had someone she could sleep near. She might not doze off, but she wouldn't be so worked up or panicked. A little voice in her head reminded her she wasn't alone.

Asher was nearby. He was downstairs, in the primary suite he'd taken her to after she'd been stung by the jellyfish. She bit down on the inside of her cheek, debating whether she was desperate enough to join him. At the next loud boom of thunder, she was out of bed and running from her room and down the stairs.

She didn't pause outside his door, either. She pushed it open and tiptoed inside. The bedroom was dark, but at the next flash of lightning, she saw him asleep on his stomach. The covers were draped over his waist, his back bare. He didn't move, not even with the next roll of thunder.

She walked around to the empty side of the bed, pulled down the covers, and slid beneath. When he still didn't twitch, not even one of those strong muscles, she relaxed and moved in closer, feeling his body heat without quite touching his skin. She lay there for a while, listening to the storm but concentrating on Asher's deep breathing, letting it lull her into a tranquil state she'd never experienced before.

★ ★ ★

ASHER WOKE UP on his back, a warm female body splayed across his chest. Nikki. How the hell had she crawled into his bed without him realizing it? And why? He'd always been a deep sleeper but to not sense her beside him?

Her head was in the crook of his arm, her body curled around his, and she had one leg bent, resting on his thigh. Her knee was too close to his groin and his very stiff erection, pressing uncomfortably against his boxer briefs.

He'd wrapped one arm around her as she slept, and when he turned his head, he inhaled her coconut-scented shampoo. Which made his dick even harder. He'd be lying if he said he hadn't wanted this to happen, even if he'd promised himself it never would.

After their day together, he'd buried himself in his office to avoid temptation. And when Derek called to check in and thank Asher again, pointing out how grateful he was that he had Asher to count on to take care of his sister, Asher knew damned well Derek wasn't thinking of *this*.

"Nikki." He spoke softly, not wanting to startle her. She didn't budge. "Nikki," he said a little louder, jostling her with his arm.

"What? Where am I?" She lifted her head and met his gaze. "Oh my God." Instead of jumping away from him, she buried her head into his shoulder and groaned.

"Why are you here?"

"It's embarrassing," she mumbled.

He shook his head. "Obviously you needed something?" he pushed.

"Yesterday I told you about my personal issues, issues with the women I model alongside. I confided in you about my direction issues and now this. You're going to think I'm a basket case."

He raised an eyebrow. "Really? Because I don't know of anyone who doesn't have problems in their life. So try me."

She still cuddled close, peeking up at him. "I have sleep problems. I always have. And I'm petrified of storms."

She ducked her head again, and he knew better than to laugh even if it wasn't *at* her problems. Just how cute she was explaining them.

Before he could reply, she lifted her head again and started to talk. "I remember when I was little, going to my parents for comfort. I walked over to my mom, wanting to snuggle with her in bed or at least get some kind of reassurance."

Asher's stomach twisted, sensing what was to come.

"My mother sent me back to my room. She told me to grow up, thunderstorms happen, and I should learn to live with it."

He was developing anger toward her parents. Why withhold love from a child when they needed it? "I'm sorry no one was there for you," he said, stroking her silky hair.

"Derek was. I used to go into his room. He had a sleeping bag and I'd curl up on the floor beside his bed. I didn't always fall asleep, but I was calmer knowing he was there."

Asher was beginning to understand the closeness these siblings shared. "So last night's storm. It was bad?"

She nodded. "Loud. I forgot my noise-cancelling headphones. They help mute the sounds. Rain was pelting the windows and the thunder shook the house. I just… couldn't be alone."

He understood. "My sister Jade has severe anxiety. Combined with migraines, she often has a hard time."

"Is that why you aren't angry I'm here? Because on some level, you get my fear?"

"Yes." He became aware of her fingers making circles on his chest… and he liked her touching him. So did his still-hard cock.

Something she hadn't realized. Yet.

She pushed herself up so she had a better view of his face. "I slept," she said, sounding amazed. "I must feel safe around you."

Did she have to say everything she felt out loud? Things he didn't want to know because it brought him closer to her in dangerous ways? Emotional ones. The kind that would let him follow his desire and not common sense.

His body was already primed. He'd inhaled her scent and felt her curves, and his heart had already softened toward this woman who just needed people to understand instead of resent her. Especially her parents.

She stirred not just Asher's desire but the protective nature he'd usually reserved for family. His father had had his hands full for so many years, Asher had just wanted to help. He'd even gone so far as to create Dirty Dare Vodka and insist they all invest, making sure everyone was set for life. His full siblings, anyway. The others had been too young. But here he was, suddenly feeling that kind of protectiveness toward Nikki.

"You're starting to get me," she murmured. "I think you may even like me. So can we agree you won't turn cold again?" Her fingers still made swirling motions on his chest, and his body liked her touch way too much.

But she was right. He both understood and like her. What she didn't comprehend was that the wall he'd put up was necessary. "Derek would kill me for not kicking you out the minute I woke up and found you here."

"But Derek isn't in charge of me. In case you've forgotten, I'm an adult."

As if he needed the reminder that legally there

wasn't a damn thing wrong with her being in his bed. Morally, when it came to his friendship with her brother, was another story. Not to mention, the age gap still made him uncomfortable. But with her fingers trailing along his skin, her head on his shoulder, and her entire body pressed up against his, he couldn't bring himself to roll over and climb out of this bed.

"Promise? You won't shut me out?" she pushed.

"Yeah," he said as he nodded, knowing he'd sealed his fate.

★ ★ ★

NIKKI LAY NESTLED between Asher's arm and warm body. The musky scent of his lingering cologne along with the muscles beneath her fingertips all worked to arouse her. She didn't doubt he felt the same way. The hitch in his breathing, the thick erection now pressing upward, showing an outline beneath the covers, said as much. But his mind was reminding him of all the reasons he believed she was wrong for him.

She intended to convince him otherwise. Something about Asher and how he treated her when he let down his guard, told her it was worth pushing him. Even if, despite how she was acting, she didn't have a ton of sexual experience.

He'd been silent since her reminder that she was of

age and there was nothing wrong with them being together. Silence that gave him time to think. She needed to distract him from his negative thoughts. She stopped making circles on his skin and walked her fingertips downward, her target obvious.

He grabbed her wrist, holding her hand in place.

Had he always been a good man who did the right thing? she wondered, her frustration mounting. But she sensed he was holding on by a thread and just needed a little more encouragement. She'd give him one more chance, and if he wasn't going to let go, she'd respect that.

"Okay," she said. The second he released his grip, she pushed herself up and maneuvered so she was straddling his waist, her arms braced on either side of his head and her sex rubbing deliciously against his cotton-covered cock.

His gaze locked with hers, his deep blue eyes turning even darker. She dipped her head so her mouth hovered over his. The need to taste him was as strong as the desire to grind herself against his straining erection.

She had the words in her head, ready to say them—*The choice is yours, Asher*– when he let out a groan and flipped their positions. She found herself beneath him, all her senses heightened by the pressure of his body and the intensity in his expression.

"Do you like to play with fire?" he asked, his tone gruff. Sexy.

"With you, I do," she said, not breaking eye contact.

He responded by sealing his lips over hers, kissing her senseless. As in, she lost all awareness of anything but Asher. His mouth devoured hers, taking everything and demanding more. He nipped at her lower lip, the shock causing her mouth to part, and he plunged his tongue inside to tangle and duel with hers. If this was Asher unleashed, she wanted whatever he was willing to give.

She threaded her fingers into his hair, holding his head in place as he continued to plunder. Every part of her body responded to his dominance. She grew lightheaded from the kiss, and a delicious ache settled low in her belly. Desire flooded her sex, and she arched her hips, grinding into him, needing more than just his mouth on hers.

He let out a low chuckle. "Trying to move things along?"

She tugged on his hair in reply. Hell yes, she was attempting to get him to do more than just kiss her.

And he did. He slipped one hand beneath her shirt and cupped her breast. His thumb rubbed back and forth over her hardening nipple, causing zings of pleasure to race through her body and settle in her core. He didn't let up, working that one tight bud until her hips were moving in faster circles, seeking relief that was just out of reach. Instead of giving her what she needed, he switched his attention to the other breast.

"Asher, please," she said, not above begging. She needed to feel him inside her. Filling her and easing the ache.

Before she could process, he shifted his big body off her and slid to the side, hooked his fingers into her skimpy panties, and yanked hard, ripping the material.

She gasped in surprise. She'd read about men ripping off a woman's underwear in books but had never experienced it in person. And it was *hot.* Especially when a man like Asher was the one as desperate for her as she was for him.

He eased his hand between her thighs, his fingers rubbing over her sex, sliding between her lips and coating her sex with her arousal.

His finger entered her, too briefly to satisfy her and she moaned, doing her best not to beg again. He lifted that same finger to his mouth, sucking it deep, and she opened her eyes wide.

And then he moved, sliding down the bed, positioning himself and pushing her thighs apart. Her knees bent without thought. He propped her legs on his shoulders, dipped his head, and took a long swipe of his tongue along her pussy before diving in and devouring her as if he'd never tasted anything so good. She saw white light and lost track of everything but the sensations shooting through her.

He knew exactly where to use that tongue to have her writhing and losing her mind. There was nowhere he didn't lick, nip, and devour. And when he began to suck on her clit, she let out a sound she didn't recognize, grinding herself against his mouth. Uncaring that she'd lost all control.

"I'm so close," she whimpered rocking against his mouth.

He raised his head and plunged one finger inside her, then two, both digits curling forward, hitting a spot she hadn't known was there. One she'd read about, but had discounted as not real. But it was. God, it was.

She whimpered, her hips moving in jerky circles, needing that one last hard thrust to send her flying.

"That's it, pretty girl. Come for me," he said before pulling her clit between his lips and sucking hard while his fingers rubbed harder inside her.

The orgasm slammed into her, waves of pleasure demanding, all-consuming, and never-ending. He didn't let up the pressure inside or out. He forced her to ride it out and, if she wasn't mistaken, be taken by a second climax before her muscles went lax and she collapsed into a shaken, sweaty mess on the bed.

★ ★ ★

FUCK.

Fuck.

Fuck. Asher ran a hand through his hair and groaned as he slid back up the mattress and lay down beside Nikki. Her face was flushed, her eyes closed, long lashes on her cheeks, and her breathing rapid.

He'd touched her.

He'd tasted her.

Made her come.

In the process, he'd broken every self-imposed promise he'd made. Derek hadn't said, *Don't touch my sister*, but his trust in sending Asher with her said as much. He'd crushed that bond, too.

He didn't have to ask himself why. From the moment he'd seen her walking toward the jet, he'd been aware of the danger. But the second he'd woken up to her in his bed, he knew he was screwed. No matter how much he'd tried to fight it, he couldn't send her away.

He couldn't even blame it on the fact that she'd deliberately baited him, though that hadn't helped. It was other things.

I slept, she'd said, sounding shocked. Then she'd

gone and added the gut punch. *I must feel safe around you,* she'd murmured. So he'd let go. He'd taken what he wanted.

And thanks to the agreement she'd extracted from him, to not turn cold and shut her out, he couldn't be a dick and treat her like shit now. Not that he would, regardless. He liked and respected her too much.

That didn't mean he wasn't beating himself up. He rolled to his side and glanced over just as her eyes opened and her gaze landed on his.

He parted his lips to speak, and she reached out, shushing him with a finger over his mouth. "Nope. Not a word. Anything you say now will only ruin something that was amazing." She lowered her hand and placed it on his hip.

A look of determination crossed her pretty face and should have put him on guard. Instead, it lit a fire inside him, one that had already been stoked when he'd gone down on her and tasted heaven.

She reached over. Slid her hand into his boxer briefs. Wrapped her fingers around his cock, and gripped him hard, swiping her thumb over the leaking head. He swallowed a groan as his hips jerked upward and her hold tightened.

A smart voice told him things had gone far enough, to stop her now, but she began to pump her hand up and down, and there wasn't a damn thing he could do but lie back and let her work her magic. He'd already been close to climaxing from her taste and the friction of his cock rubbing against the mattress minutes before. It didn't take long for him to reach that hard, ready state again, courtesy of her long fingers, solid grasp, and the little twist she added each time her palm slid down to the bottom of his shaft.

She picked up speed and things around him went fuzzy. A warning tingle surged up his spine, and his balls drew up and grew heavy. She slid down and suddenly her warm mouth surrounded him. Her tongue licked his cock and he nearly blacked out.

"Jesus, Nikki. I'm going to—"

She hollowed her cheeks, sucked harder, and sent him over the edge. His climax hit, and came long and hard. And damned if she didn't swallow every last drop.

He returned to reality to find her staring up at him, her eyes heavy lidded but her gaze wary.

"No regrets," he reassured her, before she could shush him again.

Her blinked in surprise. "Wow," she said, her lips curving upward. "That's a shock."

With a sigh, he explained. "I promised I wouldn't freeze you out again and I won't." He'd gone into this eyes open, and she'd been everything he'd wanted and more.

He could man up and admit that much. And he couldn't think of anything better than sliding inside her tight heat and fucking her senseless. He even had an uncomfortable hunch she'd be everything he wanted and more than he bargained for. But it couldn't happen.

He ran a hand through his hair. "I won't freeze you out but we can't have a repeat performance, or take things any further."

She tipped her head to the side, studying him for so long he shifted in discomfort. Finally, she must have found the answers she was seeking because she nodded. "Okay."

He narrowed his gaze. That was too easy and he hated the disappointment that filled him at her agreement.

She climbed out of bed, her tank top falling to the top of her naked bottom half. She glanced around, caught sight of a chair in the corner, and walked toward it, giving him a perfect view of her equally perfect ass.

She picked up his tee shirt strewn across the ottoman. "You don't mind, right?" Without waiting for an answer, she pulled it over her head and let it hang down to her lower thighs. "I saw there's a place to rent Jet Skis nearby?"

He nearly got whiplash at the unexpected change

of subject. She really wasn't going to fight him.

"There is. Why?"

"I think I'll ask Corey to drive me there. I'd love to rent one for an hour." She treated him to a mischievous smile, waved, and rushed out the door. No doubt to avoid dealing with his reaction, which held a heavy dose of jealousy rising to the surface.

Growling, he climbed out of bed and stalked to the bathroom so he could take a shower and be downstairs for breakfast before the little temptress could coax his hired help to drive her to her adventure.

Like it or not, Asher was going jet skiing.

★ ★ ★

NIKKI STOOD IN the shower, tipped her head back, and rinsed the conditioner out of her hair. She'd already washed up, finding herself sensitive to the touch. Memories of Asher's fingers inside her and his mouth sucking her clit as he gave her the best orgasm ever, had washed over her. And she hadn't even had sex with him yet.

Yes, yet. Because no matter how much he tried, Asher couldn't deny the chemistry between them. He wanted her as much as she desired him. But right now he needed to punish himself for what he'd done and worry about what Derek would think. To avoid an argument, she'd let Asher believe she agreed with him. No repeats. No going further.

The man was delusional. She didn't know when or who would initiate their next time, but she had no doubt they'd be tumbling into his comfortable bed again. Although she'd ace[pt him anywhere he was willing to take her, against a wall, in the shower. Bent over a table. She just wanted him.

None of these feelings or desires were familiar. She hadn't slept with Lance. Not in the biblical sense, anyway. They'd fooled around and fallen asleep together. Mostly, she'd tossed and turned. But no matter how hard he'd pressed, something had held her back from sleeping with him. They lacked the connection with him she experienced with Asher.

Even their age difference didn't bother her. Not when he understood her so well. She'd told him about her childhood, her problems, her life. Without him saying a word, a heavy warmth settled in her chest. He'd looked at her with those deep indigo eyes, and knew he understood. She'd felt the connection between them.

Why else would she sleep so well beside him, during a storm, no less?

She didn't consider herself a romantic. She had never seen two people madly in love. Her parents had an arrangement, not a love match. Her mother would remain by her father's side, raise his children, and create the perfect family for his White House run. In turn, she'd be the First Lady. Ambition first.

As for her brother, Derek hadn't fallen head over heels, to give her an example of what true love looked like, either.

All she knew was that she enjoyed being with Asher. She liked pushing his buttons, surprising him, learning about him.

And despite what he thought, she had no intention of stopping their interactions now. She had faith he'd be waiting for her downstairs to take her jet skiing, if only so she wouldn't spend the day with Corey.

She could work with that.

Chapter Six

ASHER SHOWERED AND got ready for the day. Before heading downstairs to find Nikki, he called her brother to see the status of things at home. According to him, Nikki's naked photo story had moved from the tabloids to the main newspapers, the focus less on Nikki the model and more on Nicolette Bettencourt, the potential presidential nominee's daughter. Their parents were in a state of defensive PR, trying to get control of the narrative and furious at their daughter. In other words, Nikki couldn't go home any time soon.

Knowing this whole situation wasn't her fault, Asher's anger at her parents grew. They'd left her to deal with this mess alone, uncaring that she was scared and hurt. Asher gave her credit for how strong she was, but obviously she'd learned the hard way. She only had herself to rely on. And Derek. But he wasn't here.

Asher was. So he strode out of his room and waited. He intercepted Nikki as she came down the stairs wearing a bikini with double ties on the sides and a long, unbuttoned, men's-style shirt that did nothing to hide all the bare skin beneath.

He shook his head and bit back a groan, refusing to latch onto the memories of how silky her skin felt, how wet she'd been for him, or how good she'd tasted.

"Maggie has breakfast in the kitchen," he said in a gruff voice. "Let's grab something to eat before we head out."

"We?" She eyed him with a knowing smile.

When he didn't take the bait, she shrugged.

"Sounds like a plan." She swished past him and headed for the kitchen, leaving him to grind his teeth and hope Corey wasn't in there looking for food.

A little while later, Asher found himself in the familiar shack on the beach where he often came with Zach and his siblings to enjoy a day of watersports. Although he could have his own equipment, there was something about supporting the islanders he enjoyed.

Unfortunately, the sailing company had one Jet Ski available for rental. They had two out already and another in the shop for repair.

Asher turned to Nikki. "Do you want to schedule a rental of two and come back another time?"

She shook her head. "I don't mind riding behind you. It's not like I've done this often, so it's safer for me to be the passenger. So to speak." Nikki vibrated with excitement beside him, so of course, he agreed.

"We'll take the one," Asher said to the man in board shorts, waiting for them to decide.

Which was how he found himself on a Jet Ski, Nikki holding on to him like a spider monkey, her arms wrapped tight around him. Though they both wore life vests, the entire ride still felt extremely intimate, and he liked having her close.

Water sprayed him in the face as he hit a wave and brought the machine down with the expected bump before soaring forward. Nikki screamed, then laughed, the sound echoing in his ear. Her enjoyment became his, and as he turned the Jet Ski around to head back to the rental shop, he slowed down and turned to her.

"Having fun?" he yelled over the sound of the motor.

She leaned closer, though the life vests made it difficult, and she put her chin on his shoulder. "This is the best!"

At the sound of her happiness, his heart sped up. "Hold tight!" he said and turned the handle, making the Jet Ski take off again.

He brought them back to shore, and he climbed off, helping Nikki steady herself on the beach.

She grinned. "That was incredible," she said as she squeezed the water out of her hair.

They unhooked the vests and handed them back to the shop worker.

Nikki looked around, her gaze coming to rest on a dog lying in the sand in a shady spot. "He's so cute!" She glanced at the rental guy. "Is he yours?"

He shook his head. "A stray. The island is full of them. They're called potcake dogs." He set about hanging the vests over a bar to dry.

"How did they get the name?" she asked as she stepped toward the obviously mixed-breed dog with the wagging tail.

"The name comes from a traditional Caribbean dish of seasoned rice and pigeon peas. When cooked, it leaves a cakey substance on the bottom. That's what people feed the street dogs and that's how they got their name," he said.

The golden pup, with white on its ears and nose, had shaggy, cocked ears that stuck up and folded over. He rolled over onto his back on the sand, ready for a belly rub. "Aww. Such a good"—Nikki looked between the dog's legs and laughed—"boy! Are you thirsty?" she asked.

His long tail wagged as he flipped over and stood. Nikki glanced up at Asher. "Can you go buy a bottle of water with a cap and not a squirt top? I want to give him a drink."

He looked into her pleading eyes and couldn't say no. "Be right back."

As he walked to the nearest sundry shop and purchased a bottle of water and a souvenir bowl for the *dog*, he wondered who had taken over his body and his brain. The Asher he knew wouldn't have bought a five-dollar bottle of water and a fifteen-dollar dish to feed a stray animal he'd never see again just so he could make a woman happy.

He returned to where Nikki had bent down again to pet the dog. "Thank you! Oh, good idea," she said, accepting the items and filling the bowl for the pup who immediately began to drink.

She rose to her feet and brushed the sand off her legs. "He looks hungry." She nibbled on her lower lip, her worry obvious.

Bad enough she was still in the skimpy bikini, but now Asher had to watch her slick her tongue over where she'd bitten, making him want to taste her mouth again. Not to mention other delicious parts.

He let out a groan. "Let's grab our towels, dry off, and get something for lunch."

"But—" Her gaze slid back to the dog. "Can we bring him back food? Please?"

Her lashes fluttered and not in a coy way, either. He saw her heart revealed in her eyes. "Okay. How about we get burgers and bring one back for him?"

"Thank you!" She squealed and threw her arms around his neck, pressing her body against his. "Deep down you're a softie," she said, brushing her lips over his. “Thanks again.”

She put space between them and acted as if she hadn’t just kissed him. And not on the cheek, either. She walked toward the table where they’d left their shirts and other things under the watchful eye of the owner, clearly expecting Asher to follow.

Which he did. He was learning the woman could be a force when she wanted to be. Restaurants were within walking distance of the beach and they headed to the shops and eateries.

They had hamburgers at a standing table, and as they finished, they talked about life. “Do you like modeling?” he asked, knowing he had an innate bias against the profession because of his ex.

“Hmm. I can tell by your tone you don’t approve of the career choice and we’ll get to that in a minute. But to answer your question, not really. It made sense for me to take that path. My mother had forced me into pageants, and then she wanted me to model. I didn’t particularly want to but I needed money if I was going to get away from my parents. It was something I could do in my mid to late teens to start saving.” She shrugged and took a sip of her soda. “By the time Derek moved to Manhattan, I was already traveling abroad for work, so I convinced them to let me live there, too.”

“That must have been a relief.” He couldn’t imagine how stifled she felt traveling alone, then coming home to her difficult parents with their high expectations.

"It was. But I don't love it. It's competitive, and the girls I've met are mean, manipulative, and out for themselves."

He crumpled the paper from his burger. "Hmm. What would you do? If you had the choice?"

She looked at him as if no one had ever asked her that before. Perhaps no one had.

"I'm not sure. When my neighbor, Winter, a journalist, told me that she was interviewing your brother, Harrison, and his partners about their production company, I felt a flutter of excitement." She shrugged and crinkled up her garbage. "I'm intrigued by what happens early in the process of movie making and what goes on behind the scenes. But I have no experience and I didn't graduate from college so..."

"So when you go home, I'll introduce you to Harrison and see how he can help you."

"Really? You'd do that for me?" she asked, eyes lit up with excitement.

"Of course. You're smart. Don't let whatever your parents said make you think otherwise." He had no doubt they'd belittled her and put her in a small box to try to control her.

Her eyes warmed at his comment. "They used to

say it's a good thing I was pretty because I couldn't rely on my smarts. You know, I got the beauty, Derek got the brains." She let out a derisive snort.

"Not true. I remember our talk on the trip here and how you quickly focused on market strategy. By concentrating on your beauty, they denied your intelligence. It's shameful," he muttered.

She grinned. "I like how you really do understand what my childhood was like. How it's shaped me." Tipping her head to one side, she studied him. "But you haven't given me nearly as much about you. So… let's hear it."

He grabbed their wrappers and empty soda cups and walked to the nearest trash can, throwing out the garbage. He returned to her, well aware she wouldn't let him wriggle out of answering her questions.

"Let's hear what?" Because he wasn't about to just spill all his family and personal secrets. She'd need to be specific.

She tapped one slender finger on her cheek. "Let's start with why you dislike models so much. I'm pretty sure whatever the reason, it helped contribute to your negative feelings about me. Before you got to know me, of course."

Picking up the bag with the stray's meal, she said, "Let's walk back to the dog while you tell me what I want to know. I'm sure Lucky is hungry."

Oh, shit. She'd named the dog. He was sure that didn't bode well for him in the long run. Suddenly he'd rather talk about his past relationships than let her focus on a dog she couldn't have.

"I assume you've heard of Christy Baylor?" he asked as he strode along the sandy sidewalk, Nikki by his side.

"Yes! She was *the* face of some major brands," she said, excited. "I don't know her personally, she's older than me, but she's had a wonderful career. I idolize how she's managed herself."

He drew a deep breath and let it out. "As long as you don't idolize her personality," he muttered.

Nikki placed a hand on his arm and they stopped walking. "What did she do to you?" she asked, her voice soft.

He ran a hand over his face and groaned. "Okay, look. I've had two long-term relationships in my life." She might as well hear it all. "The first one was in business school. Mara. We had similar goals and spent a ton of time together before I met your brother and Knox. Mara and I were together for six months. I thought I was in love. One night, I surprised her at her apartment. Her roommate let me in, and I walked into Mara's room as she was telling her parents she was sure she had me wrapped around her finger. She assured them that, by the time we graduated, we'd get married, I'd be paying off her school loans, and she'd set them all up for life. Turns out she'd targeted me from day one."

He still kicked himself for being duped.

Nikki's eyes narrowed and an angry expression he'd never seen crossed her face. "Can I claw her eyes out for you?" she asked.

He shook his head and let out a chuckle. "Easy, tiger. I don't even know what happened to her. I dumped her and never spoke to her again." But he couldn't deny he liked how pissed Nikki was on his behalf.

"So she made you distrust women's motives," she astutely said. "That's something we have in common. And Christy, the model?"

"Caught her having sex with her yoga teacher." He tried to shrug it off but couldn't deny the betrayal still stung. Not because he'd loved her but he hated having been made a fool of.

"Cheaters are horrible human beings," Nikki muttered. "But cheating on *you*? That makes her a moron, as well."

He raised his brows, unable to believe that one short statement took away the sting. And bolstered his ego at the same time.

He laughed and met her gaze. "You're special, Nikki. Always remember that. Now let's get that dog fed." Grasping her hand, he led her back to the water sports shop.

★ ★ ★

BY THE TIME they returned, the dog had disappeared. Nikki wasn't just disappointed, she was worried. He'd seemed so thin and she'd been able to feel his ribs when she petted him. And the way he'd consumed the water, he was obviously thirsty, too.

"The dog walked toward the parking lot," the shop guy said.

Nikki forced a smile. "Thank you." Unwilling to leave the burgers in case she saw him on her way to the car, she held the bag in her hand.

"There are thousands of strays and you can't save them all," Asher said, obviously sensing her thoughts and her mood. He placed a hand on her back, guiding her toward where they'd parked the SUV.

Normally she'd be thinking about the fact that Asher had opened up about his romantic history, but that dog and its sweet face stayed with her. She'd just have to think more about what he'd said and how it had impacted him later.

They stepped into the lot and Asher hit the key fob, causing the SUV nearby to beep as the doors unlocked.

Nikki took a step and heard a bark. She turned and there he was. "Lucky!"

She'd named him because when she'd found him, she'd given him water and had planned to feed him, too. So he'd gotten lucky. And now she was convinced she'd given him the right name.

The dog turned at the sound of her voice.

Ignoring Asher's groan, a sound he made often around her, she knelt down by the car and opened the bag, pulling out the food. Two burgers, not one. She grinned. Asher was more of a softy than he liked to let on.

Lucky bounded over, and she rose to her feet, watching as

the pup ate the plain patties – so fast it was obvious he'd been starving.

"I left his water and dish by the sports shed," she said, glancing at Asher.

With a sigh, he shook his head and pulled them out of the bag she hadn't noticed he'd taken with him. Grinning, she poured water into the bowl and let the dog go to town. After he finished, she cleaned up and put all the garbage along with the bowl back into the bag.

Full and obviously grateful, the dog leaned against her leg, and she glanced up at Asher. She'd never been the kind of girl to flutter her lashes and act coy to get what she wanted, but if there was ever a time, this was it.

She widened her eyes and met Asher's gaze. "He needs me."

"Nikki, no. Come on, he's covered in sand and who knows what else. Getting a dog off the island is complicated."

"But not impossible, right?" She deliberately fluttered her lashes.

"Cut it out," he muttered.

She bit down on the inside of her cheek. "Please?"

"That dog is not getting in my car."

He said the words but there was no heat behind them, so she opened the back door and Lucky jumped inside.

She shut him in and turned to Asher with a wide, happy, grateful smile. "What's that you were saying?"

He rolled his eyes but still opened her door like the gentleman he was. A few minutes later, they were on their way back to the estate, Asher mumbling something about pushy women, needing to find a vet, and getting the damned dog a bath before he gave them all fleas.

But the person who'd been hurt twice, who'd clearly hardened himself against women and relationships, had shown her the man he really was.

And she liked everything she'd seen.

★ ★ ★

ASHER HOPPED OUT of the Rover, hoping Maggie would put an end to this stray dog thing, since he'd obviously been a pussy. He'd taken one look at Nikki's pleading eyes, and despite knowing she was deliberately playing him, he'd given in when he could have forced the dog back out of the SUV. But he couldn't do it. Not to the happy, tail-wagging, dog and especially not to a grinning Nikki.

He didn't recognize himself. Not one damned bit.

He needed Maggie to take one look at the dirty animal and refuse to let him into the house. Asher would find a rescue place on the island to give him to, and he'd spend time comforting Nikki. Would he feel like shit about it? Yes. But it was the right thing to do.

Except the minute they stepped into the house and Maggie met them at the door, she took one look at the mutt and her eyes warmed. "You poor baby! Where did you find him?"

"On the beach," Nikki said. "He's so hungry and thirsty. I already gave him water and burgers but—"

"He needs a bath next." Maggie pulled out her cell and hit a button, then put the phone to her ear. "Corey? I need you to take a trip into town. I'll send you a list of pet supplies I need."

Then Asher watched in shocked silence as his

housekeeper and the woman who was changing him in not subtle ways walked off together, dog following them.

Shaking his head and knowing he was outnumbered, he let them go. He needed a shower, too. Afterwards, he pulled out his laptop and researched what they needed to let them travel home with a dog. Information found, he then searched for the name of a vet on the island. If Nikki was going to take the dog to the States, he needed an exam for a certificate of veterinary inspection, a rabies shot, and an ISO-compatible microchip.

He paid the vet a hefty fee to stay open late and fit them in as his last appointment after his normal business hours, which gave Asher and Nikki time to eat dinner first. If he didn't get the paperwork and vet check done, Nikki would lose that happy smile and she'd worry about being forced to leave Lucky here when it came time to leave. And Asher had already come to the conclusion he liked seeing her happy.

What he didn't understand was why he cared so damned much. This was supposed to be a favor for a friend. A babysitting job. One where he looked out for Derek's sister until the tabloid shit blew over and she could go home. Instead, he was getting closer to her, confiding in her, letting her into his bed. And now making sure she could keep the dog she'd fallen in love with. All because he liked being the one to put that genuine smile on her face.

He stepped out of his bedroom and walked toward the kitchen, wondering if he'd find the dog roaming around the house. Instead, he discovered Lucky in the kitchen where he happily gnawed on a chew toy. Bowls of dry food and water had been placed in an out-of-the-way spot, and a leash hung over the doorknob on the French doors leading to the patio.

Nikki, Maggie, and Corey were talking near the center island. And since Nikki's focus was solely on her new pet, Asher couldn't bring himself to care that Corey was there, too.

Nikki had showered and left her damp hair in two long braids hanging on either side of her head. With no makeup, she was fresh-faced and beautiful, giving him no doubt why she succeeded in the modeling world. There was something inherently natural about her. Sweet, with the ability to hold her own. Though he knew how rocky her life was, both at home and within her career, she amazed him with her ability to be cheerful most of the time and to instill that same positive feeling in others.

"Asher, come in," Maggie said, noticing him in the entryway. "Dinner will be ready soon."

"I told Maggie we should eat inside." Nikki glanced at him. "I don't want Lucky wandering off.

Once he's microchipped, we can see how he does outside without a leash. If he stays nearby or wanders."

"Makes sense to me." He walked in and joined them, nodding at Corey, who was munching on a carrot.

"I was asking Maggie if she knew anything about vets on the island, but she's never needed one so she doesn't know." Nikki glanced at the dog and her gaze softened.

"Already handled," Asher said. "We have an appointment at seven p.m. Dr. Young is willing to see Lucky after what would have been his last patient for the night."

Her eyes opened wide. "Thank you! I didn't expect… Never mind. Just thank you."

He chuckled, not surprised at her reaction. He hadn't been on board bringing the dog home. "You're welcome."

Asher settled onto a stool and made himself comfortable. A crudités plate sat in the center the countertop. He picked up a yellow pepper, dipped it in hummus, and took a bite.

Corey glanced at his mother. "I'm out. I have a date," he told her, and since the man was now off the clock, it was none of Asher's business.

"Have fun," she said.

"Thanks. Night, Mr. Dare, Nikki."

"Bye, Corey. Thanks for picking up everything for Lucky. I really appreciate it." Nikki treated him to a beaming smile, but for once, Asher's stomach didn't twist with jealousy.

"I'll be back. I want to check on dinner." Maggie disappeared into the main kitchen, where the chef had more room to cook for guests, since Asher's large family often came to the island together.

The family-style kitchen where they now sat was for casual gatherings. And if his mom or anyone wanted to cook for themselves, they could do it here. Asher had gone all out with this house, wanting everyone to have what they needed.

He took a moment to study Nikki. She wore ripped jean shorts and a flowing pink top, her tanned skin shimmering beneath the lights overhead. Then again, it could be his imagination. He just liked looking at her.

"I need to pay Corey back for the dog supplies. He really went overboard and I'm so grateful," she said, pulling up a stool near Asher's and sitting down.

He shook his head. "I gave him the list and he paid with my credit card. Consider it a gift."

"That's … wow. Thank you." She paused. "This from the man who didn't want the dog in his car?" She met his gaze, curiosity dancing in her eyes as a slight crinkle appeared above her nose.

Asher chuckled. "You have to admit we had no idea what was living in his fur."

"Eew. Well, we gave him a good bath and the vet can look him over tonight. As for the car, I suppose you can have it washed?"

He nodded. "I already had someone take care of it."

"I'm not shocked." She propped her elbows on the island and her chin on her hands. "So, I was doing some googling about what I'd need to do to bring Lucky home with me. He needs a rabies shot and certificate, which I'm sure he can get tonight, and an ISO-compatible microchip, which I'm also hoping can be done by the vet."

"The doctor can do it all. I've already asked and confirmed with him on the phone when I made the appointment. And since the Bahamas isn't a high-risk country for rabies, you don't need to wait thirty days after vaccination to bring him into the United States. You'll be fine whenever it's time to leave," he assured her.

She sat up straight and stared at him, her mouth opened in surprise. "You—"

"Took care of it, yes." He placed his hand under her chin and pushed her jaw closed, chuckling as he did.

"But… But… you didn't want the dog here."

"I never said that, exactly. It just wasn't part of the plan. You took me off guard." Something she seemed to do regularly. "Anyway, I want you to be happy and Lucky does that for you."

"Dinner is ready!" Maggie called out from the other room before Nikki could react to Asher's unplanned admission. He'd never meant to confess to those feelings out loud.

Since Nikki still seemed to be in shock, he stood, grasped her hand, and tugged her to her feet. "Come on. Let's eat so we can get to the vet."

★ ★ ★

LUCKY'S APPOINTMENT WENT well, though Asher admitted to holding his breath while he waited for the dog to get a clean bill of health. Although they wouldn't get blood work and *other* samples back for a day or two, the vet said the dog was in decent shape for a street pup.

He was skinny but had obviously been fed by restaurant workers who'd probably kept an eye on him and the other strays, feeding them leftovers and scraps, as was common practice. Unlike some others he'd seen who'd been abused.

The vet gave her better food than what Corey had

picked up. Lucky had received his shots and appeared to be in as good of health as they could hope for. She'd have to follow up with a vet once they returned to New York.

By the time they made it back home, it had been a long day. They walked Lucky until he did his business and brought him inside.

She held his leash and stopped by the stairs. "Asher, I can't thank you enough. Today has been so many things. Surprising, for sure, finding him, taking him with me. But you've made it possible and I'm so grateful."

"Don't be. You deserve to have someone do something good for you without expecting anything in return."

She tipped her head to the side, studying him as the dog rubbed against her legs. "Who does those kinds of things for you?"

He swallowed, the question hitting hard, though he knew from her tone of voice she hadn't meant it as a dig. Just the opposite.

"I have my family."

"And you're fortunate but that's not what I meant." She pulled him into a spontaneous hug, her cheek pressed against his. "Thanks again," she said, turning to go upstairs.

Which left Asher with a choice. Do the smart

thing, let her go to sleep in her room, and keep pushing her away? Or call her back, invite her in, and give in to what they both wanted for as long as it could last. For whatever time was left here on the island.

★ ★ ★

"NIKKI, WAIT." ASHER'S words took Nikki by surprise, and she spun around, the dog halting on the step above her.

Asher had walked to the edge of the staircase. "You," he said. "You do that for me. You're here because you have to be, but you're pushing me out of my comfort zone. And you're showing me life can be fun if I let myself relax and stop trying to control everything."

She couldn't help but laugh. "Can you do that?"

He grinned, a sexy smile that melted her inside. "I'm working on it."

"I'm glad." Warmth spread through her at his words.

He was doing her a huge favor by having her here, not to mention allowing her new dog to stay and going out of his way to make sure she could bring Lucky home. But to know she was giving something valuable to Asher in return? That was important to her.

"Are you going to sneak into my room tonight?"

he asked.

She gripped the stair handle hard. "Do you want me to?" Her heart seemed to rise to her throat.

It was one thing to crawl into his bed when she'd been scared. And though she'd been touchy with him throughout the day, kissing him when she felt like it, she didn't have a seduction planned. He'd pulled away often enough that she needed him to extend the invitation and admit he wanted her first.

"Come." He extended his hand, and she looked up and along the leash to the patient pup. For a street dog, he was such a good boy. "His crate and bed and things are set up in my room," she said, glancing back at Asher.

He raised an eyebrow. "I'm not having sex with a dog watching me." An amused expression settled on his face, lips lifted as he shook his head.

She let out a loud laugh. She wouldn't want that, either. "I'll settle him in the crate and come down once I know he's quiet."

And after Asher fell asleep, she'd bring the dog into his room so she could keep an eye on him *and* stay the night in Asher's bed.

"I'll be waiting," he said in a gruff voice, and when she glanced down, she saw the outline of his erection through his cargo shorts.

"Asher?"

"Yes?"

She drew a deep breath. "What are we doing?"

He blew out a rough sigh. "Enjoying each other while we're on the island. Can you do that?"

She nodded, ignoring the drop in her stomach. She might not agree with his reasons why they couldn't have more but neither would she miss out on what he was offering. And if a part of her hoped he'd come around when their time here ended? She'd just have to get over the disappointment when that didn't happen.

Knowing he expected an answer, she looked into his handsome face and nodded. "Yeah. I can do that."

Relief washed over his tense facial muscles and he actually smiled. "Good. Now hurry up and come to my bed."

His need inspired her own, and she rushed up the stairs to take care of the dog and shower so she could get back to Asher. Before he had too much time to think and changed his mind.

Chapter Seven

WHILE NIKKI WAS handling the dog, Asher went to his room. He walked to the bed, turned down the sheet and comforter, and settled on top to wait.

He had no intention of overthinking things, deciding his usual MO wouldn't work when it came to Nikki. He was done waffling. He was all in. For now. As all in as he could be with a woman whose time on the island had an end date, even if he didn't know how soon that day would come. He'd deal with the repercussions of diving into a relationship with her later, both with her and with her brother.

Luckily, he didn't have to wait long for her to arrive. One light knock and Nikki entered his room, stepping inside and shutting the double doors behind her. Her long tee shirt hit mid-thigh, leaving her tanned legs bare. That same thin cotton made her hardened nipples show through the sheer fabric, and his mouth watered at the thought of taking each one into his mouth.

She walked toward him but stopped halfway across the room and studied him, eyes wide, as if she expected him to change his mind and ask her to leave. He'd certainly sent enough mixed messages since they'd met for her concern to be valid.

He crooked a finger. "Get over here," he said, leaving no doubt about his intentions.

She stepped over to the bed, her gaze darkening as she looked at his erect cock threatening to burst through his boxer briefs. He had no intention of hiding what she did to him. Instead, he pushed his underwear down his legs and kicked them off. Naked now, he gripped his erection in his hand and squeezed, gliding his palm up and down, stoking his desire.

Nikki stared at the display. She licked her lips, then reached for the hem of her shirt and pulled it over her head, revealing her bra-less breasts and, when she removed her silk shorts, her lack of underwear beneath.

The sight made his own mouth water. He'd already tasted her pussy and licked her through her climax, yet the sight of her beautiful curves and neatly trimmed sex set him on fire.

"You better not have run into anyone on your way here." Normally, nobody wandered the house at night, but he didn't want Corey getting a glimpse of what belonged to Asher. Jesus fuck. That was taking things too far. He was better off focusing on having her now.

She shook her head, her hair flowing over her

shoulders. "Nope. I didn't see a soul."

"Good. Now get up here."

Naked, she put one knee on the mattress and pushed herself up. He grasped her beneath her arms and pulled her on top of him, her warm body covering his. He gave himself a second to enjoy the feel of her curves fitting perfectly against his harder muscles and to focus on the light kisses she pressed along his jaw.

Though he'd planned to be the one tasting, her tongue traced a path along his neck, then collarbone before moving lower. She nuzzled his chest with her nose and lips before she licked and circled first one of his nipples, bringing it to a hard peak, before starting on the other.

Pleasure took hold and his hips jerked, desire coiling inside him. He wrapped her hair in his fist and tugged. "Come on up, Nikki. I have plans for you."

Instead of complying, she placed a hand on his chest and held him in place. "Nope. It's my turn," she said, eyes glittering, the enjoyment she took in her actions obvious. She went back to her torment, wrapping her tongue around his nipple once more.

His body throbbed, the need to bury himself inside her clawing at him. "Payback's a bitch," he warned her, treating her to another hard tug on her hair until she let out a strangled moan.

But undeterred, she went back to kissing and licking him, creating a cool, wet trail down the center of his abdomen, her direction clear. At this point, he needed to feel her warm mouth suck him deep, and he clenched his free fist at his side as she stroked her tongue across the head of his cock. Once, then twice before her mouth consumed him completely.

Jesus.

She felt so good as she gripped the base of his shaft and ran her hand up and down his long length. His hips rose and fell along with the slick glide of her palm and the cushioned heat of her mouth. A low hum sounded from the back of her throat, then a vibration raced through him and he thrust his cock deeper.

A warning tingle raced up his spine, and he slammed one hand against the mattress, gritting his teeth. "No."

She released him with a pop and looked up, meeting his gaze. "Problem?"

She was such an adorable brat. Her attitude had him growing harder, something he hadn't thought possible.

Which brought him back to his point. "When I come, it's going to be in your pussy, not your mouth, and you'll be climaxing right along with me."

"Oh." Her eyes, wide and green as fresh grass, glazed with need. "Sounds like a plan," she said, crawling to the head of the bed and turning around.

She leaned against the pillows beside him, and he reached for his nightstand, pulling a condom from the drawer. He ripped open the wrapper and rolled it on before rising up and straddling her hips.

Unexpected and unwanted thoughts intruded, the reasons he shouldn't be with her trying to crowd into his head, giving rise to second thoughts. Then she curled her smaller hand around his cock and swiped her thumb over the head. From that moment on, nothing mattered but Nikki.

★ ★ ★

NIKKI STARED AT Asher, taking in his handsome, masculine features. From the beard that had grown fuller since they'd been on the island to his strong jaw, the dark hair falling over his forehead, and deep, sensual gaze, he was her idea of perfection. She hadn't thought they'd get to this point, but now that they had, she wanted everything from him.

Those words, that promise, made in his gruff, rumbling voice, affected her on a level that frightened her. She'd never been as comfortable as she was with Asher. She could act like herself, not feel self-conscious, even naked. The appreciation showed in his gaze.

She hadn't slept with her last boyfriend, despite his pressure, because deep down, something had felt off. That she'd come to Asher's bed and wanted him inside her told her this thing between them meant something, at least to her.

A look of concern flashed over his face, his eyes drifting away from her. He sat upright, his thick erection gripped in his hand, and despite her sudden worry, her sex clenched with desire.

"What is it?" she asked.

He shook his head, as if shaking off whatever he'd been thinking.

"It's all good."

"Okay." Staring at his rigid erection, she licked her lips, his taste still on her tongue.

"You're a tease," he said in a gruff voice. And as if in retaliation, he grazed the head of his cock over her sex, rubbing her clit hard enough to send sparks of desire rushing through her body, without the pressure and friction she needed to come.

"So are you." She pouted in the hopes he'd satisfy them both. "*Please*, Asher."

A grin lifted his sexy lips. "Please what?"

"Please hurry." She raised her hips, giving him a glimpse of how wet and ready for him she was.

His eyes darkened and he slid his fingers through her slick juices, easing one long digit inside her. Her body immediately tightened around him, and a wave of need hit her hard.

"So good," she murmured, arching her hips, taking him deeper, and squeezing her inner walls around him.

He pumped his finger in and out, and she moved her hips up and down to the rhythm he set. Before she could get used to the sensation of him dragging inside her, he pulled out and rubbed his cock along her pussy, the head teasing her clit *again.* A delicious surge of arousal washed over her, more intense with each pass of his erection over her sex, but it still wasn't enough.

"*Please, Asher.* I need you," she begged, and he caved, notching himself at her entrance and sliding in a little before coming to a stop.

He held himself there, his arms shaking beside her. She let out a low, frustrated moan and squeezed around him, hoping to drag him in deeper. She couldn't take the way he inched inside her, pushing in, then halting just as her inner muscles began to clench, searching for something just out of reach. She arched her back, her hips shook, but he was still depriving her of the fullness she desired.

Tears formed in her eyes. "Quit teasing me, Asher."

His expression softened and he leaned down, licking at the tear that had escaped. "I'm sorry. I just want to make sure you're ready for me," he said, sweat beading on his brow.

She rolled her eyes, unsure whether to be touched or annoyed. "I'm not a virgin, you know."

A muscle pulsed in his jaw at her admission. "I assumed but you are so fucking tight and, you feel so good, I just want to slam into you hard. But I don't want to hurt you," he said, voice softening, lips brushing over hers.

With their bodies aligned and his cock still partway inside her, it was frustrating, yes, but at the same time, so sweet and intimate. So unlike the Asher she'd met at the airport and more like the man she was coming to know.

She kissed his chin and breathed in his scent, drowning in how perfect he smelled.

"You're okay?" he asked, gliding out and pushing back into her, arms shaking, as he barely held on to his restraint.

"I am but I know how I could be better." And in case he needed an explanation, she squeezed her inner muscles around him.

He took the hint and thrust into her completely, letting out a satisfied groan. "F-u-ck, Nikki. So fucking good."

She agreed, as her entire being lit up from the inside out. He was huge, stretching her insides, but it was perfect. Pleasure consumed her and she dug her nails into his shoulders, not caring if she broke skin. Heaven couldn't feel this perfect, she thought.

Until he began to move and she soared even higher, letting herself go and experience all that was Asher. He pumped his hips, moving inside her, each pass in and out harder than the one before.

"Look at me."

She did.

And he stared into her eyes as he continued to take her. The slapping noise of skin against skin, the slickness of their bodies connecting were the most erotic sounds she'd ever heard. But it was more than sexual. Her soul connected to his and he filled the empty spaces that had lived inside her all of her life.

She had to face facts. He owned her body. No man would ever come close to the feel of Asher inside her.

She wrapped her legs around his hips. The new angle brought him deeper, and he rubbed against just the right spot inside her. White spots flashed behind her eyes and fire licked at her veins.

"That's it, Nikki. Come for me."

"I am. Oh God, I am." She blanked out everything but sensation.

And Asher? He held on, driving into her as she rode out a climax that seemed to never end.

Only when she began to come down from the high

did he let go and chase his own pleasure. A few more thrusts gave her mini aftershocks, and then he stiffened above her, coming with a harsh groan, her name on his lips.

★ ★ ★

ASHER WOKE UP to a feeling of déjà vu and Nikki's body half covering his. Only this time, he knew exactly how he'd ended up in this position. He could get used to waking up to her draped over him every morning. The thought caught him off guard. He wasn't a man who wanted a woman in his bed for more than a night or two, max. And her bed was preferrable. He definitely didn't want to wake up to a female and give her the wrong idea.

Yet here he was, thinking about Nikki and… No. He wasn't going to delve into it any more than he would overthink the consequences of his actions. He was relaxed and intended to stay that way. Without opening his eyes, he slid his arm down her bare back, cupped one ass cheek in his hand, and squeezed. He slipped his finger lower and toyed with her sex, feeling her grow wet around him.

"You're up early," she practically slurred. "Two rounds weren't enough for you?"

He grinned at the reminder of what had been the

best sex of his life. Something else he wouldn't be overanalyzing, because he had no desire to dig into what that meant, either.

"Consider the first time an appetizer, the second, my main course." Since he'd made her come with his mouth before burying himself inside her body, the metaphor made sense. "This morning we can call it dessert."

A warm tongue licked his temple. *Not* on the side where Nikki still lay snuggled on top of him.

He opened his eyes, came face-to-face with the dog, and groaned. "What happened to crate training?" he muttered, moving Lucky's face and open mouth away from his.

Nikki shrugged against him, her body still loose, obviously not the least bit repentant. "After you fell asleep, I walked him again because I don't know his habits. Then I felt guilty bringing him upstairs to be alone in an unfamiliar room, locked in a crate, when he's used to being free."

She slid her palm over Asher's chest and rubbed the skin above his heart in an obvious attempt to soften him up.

He glanced at the dog, who now lay on his other side, the two of them making a sandwich of his body. "But he's in my bed."

"Lucky had a bath, remember? And he's such a

good boy, you had no idea he even spent the night here." Nikki popped her head up and met his gaze, her eyes sparkling with amusement. "I notice you haven't moved your hand."

She wiggled her butt against his palm. What could he say? He enjoyed cupping one perfect ass cheek. "I like it there."

But he released her and rose, causing the dog to hop to the floor. "I'm going to walk him and I'll be right back." He gave her ass a light slap.

She squealed. "Asher!"

Chuckling, he slipped on a pair of shorts and led the dog to the bedroom door. A glance back showed him Nikki, head on the pillow, blanket half off, one long leg sticking out. She looked good there, and he could get used to having her naked, in his personal space. There it was. Those unnerving thoughts again.

What was he doing? His friend would murder him and there was no doubt things between Asher and Nikki were already messy. He never let emotion into his sex life but he'd wanted to see her eyes when he was inside her, when he made her come. If it meant something to him, he had no doubt Nikki would get invested as well.

And then what? He didn't fucking know. But no matter what, he needed to treat her with care and think about her feelings before his own.

Shaking off questions he had no answers for, he opened the door and Lucky trotted out ahead of him. He planned to let the dog out the side door and wait for him to do his thing and come back. He wasn't stupid enough to let Nikki's new pet disappear.

"There you are!" Maggie exclaimed. Ignoring Asher, she bent down to rub the dog's head. "Come. Let's go out and then get you something to eat."

She rose and started for the kitchen. "Oh!" She turned to face Asher. "Why do I have the feeling you forgot your family is arriving today?"

"What?" He blinked at her words.

"Yes, I had a hint when you weren't up early that they were the last thing on your mind. And yesterday was so busy with the dog…" Her voice trailed off. "Anyway, it's your parents' anniversary? Everyone is coming… well, whoever isn't pregnant or away at school." She chuckled at that. "You're distracted. I wonder why?" she mused knowingly.

They both knew why.

Dammit. He'd been so consumed with first avoiding Nikki, then watching and hanging out with her, always wanting her, he'd forgotten everything else.

At least it was a small group arriving. Jade was in the early stages of her pregnancy and preferred to stay close to home. Nick's wife was also pregnant, and they'd decided not to pack up their six-year-old daughter and travel for the short weekend. In a family as large as theirs, it was rare to get everyone in one place at the same time.

"I'll go tell Nikki," he said, mentally preparing himself for the onslaught.

"Don't worry. You have some time before they descend on you," Maggie reassured him before she strode off, talking to Lucky as she headed for the kitchen.

He groaned and ran his fingers through his hair, walking back into the bedroom and closing the door.

Nikki appeared more awake than she had earlier. She'd put her sleep shirt back on and sat up in bed. "Where's Lucky?"

Asher slid in beside her. "Maggie's walking and feeding him."

"She's such an easygoing, sweet woman. While we were giving Lucky his bath, she mentioned she used to work for your family?"

Wanting her close and refusing to question why, Asher pulled Nikki against him. He liked their cocoon and decided to steal more time before telling her they were having company. Once his parents and siblings arrived, there'd be no more alone time, and he'd have to deal with a reality that would be just like their return to the city.

His stomach twisted at the thought of their time

being over. Fuck, he'd done a one-eighty on his feelings.

"Asher? Are you okay?" Nikki asked.

He nodded, forcing himself to focus on her question. It was better for her to have the Dare family history before she met everyone. "Maggie is amazing," he agreed. "She held down the fort along with my stepmother, Serenity. My family is... *large*." Bigger than the Brady Bunch. "Did Derek ever tell you about us?"

Nikki shook her head.

"Where should I start?" he asked aloud.

"The beginning always makes the most sense." She curled her legs beneath her.

Asher didn't tell many people about his childhood. He definitely had never confided in the women he dated. Sure, he'd explained to both Mara and Christy because he'd believed he could trust them. He'd been wrong in his assessment, but he'd grown since then and trusted his judgment. He'd jumped to conclusions about Nikki before getting to know her. Now he did. And Asher was no longer wrong about her.

"My biological mother's name was Audrey. She married my father, Michael, and they immediately had kids. Me first. Then Harrison, Zach, and the twins, Nick and Jade." He leaned against the pillows, rubbing at his chest. Bringing up these old memories wasn't easy.

"You said Audrey *was* your biological mother?" Beside him, Nikki shifted until she was more comfortable.

Asher nodded and blew out a harsh breath. The lump in his throat that always accompanied telling this story had returned. "She died by suicide when I was nine."

"Oh, Asher." Nikki didn't grasp his hand as a friend would do. No, she climbed right into his lap and wrapped her arms around him, holding him tight. "I'm so sorry." Her breath was warm near his ear, and she pressed her cheek to his.

For the first time in his life, he allowed himself to accept comfort. He hugged her back, breathing in the remnants of her coconut shower gel before shifting her so she sat in his lap and he could continue his story.

But she clutched his hand and kept her fingers curled tightly around his. "Only if you want to tell me more," she said, obviously not wanting to push.

"I do." He squeezed her hand back in reassurance. "My mother had emotional issues. She was neglectful. To hear Dad tell it, she liked being pregnant and sought out the attention that came with it, but she just didn't take care of me. After Harrison was born, Dad hired a nanny and Serenity came to live with us. I was about three years old at the time."

Nikki didn't say a word, she just waited for more, making it easier for Asher to explain.

He swallowed hard. "Nothing happened between Serenity and my father while my parents were together." He dipped his head as he explained. "But kids can be brutal. The ones who like to tease, bully, and make fun of something they either don't understand or think will get laughs."

Nikki put a hand on his back and rubbed gently. "So I take it your dad and the nanny thing was hard for you?"

"Hot young woman moves in with a married couple? Then the man's wife runs off and they're alone together playing house? And later they marry? Yes, you could say it was hard. But as much as those memories are there and they suck? Serenity is the only mother most of my siblings really remember."

Nikki shifted in his lap, and her bare lower half rubbed against him.

"You're making it hard to concentrate on having a conversation," he said, not at all bothered by that fact.

She wriggled, her damp sex grinding into his cock. "You're right. It's hard." Her eyes sparkled with both desire and amusement, making him smile.

Something else she brought out in him.

"But you need to get this off your chest." She slid

off, retaking her position beside him, legs crossed, pulling the covers over her waist. "As much as I'd like to act on… *that*"—she tipped her head toward his erection—"I want to know about you more," she said, meeting his gaze.

A woman wanting to understand him more than she desired him or something he could give her? Well, that was different.

"Your siblings consider Serenity their mom, but you were old enough to remember your mother, right?" Nikki asked.

He groaned. "Which means I remember her neglect."

"But also her love?" Nikki intuitively asked. For someone so young, she had a remarkable depth of understanding.

Loving and missing his mom wasn't something Asher thought about often, but he supposed Nikki had a point. "You're right. I remember that, too. Which makes it complicated. A part of me would feel guilty calling Serenity Mom, not that she ever asked me to."

"Well, that's good."

"It is. And I believe I came to terms with it all, especially once there were more kids. My half siblings."

Nikki's eyes opened wide, her curiosity piqued. "How many more of you *are* there?"

He grinned. "There are the triplets. They're nineteen. And Layla, the oops baby later. She's fourteen."

"Wow. No wonder you're the serious one. As the oldest, I bet you see it as your duty to look out for everyone. I mean, Derek just has me to worry about, and *he* takes overprotective to the extreme." Nikki rose to her knees and cupped her hands around Asher's face, looking deep into his eyes. "Who looks out for *you*?"

She'd asked him a similar question last night except his answer today went deeper and made him feel vulnerable, something he generally avoided.

Who wanted to admit the answer was no one looked out for him? Sure, his siblings loved him and would be there if he needed them, but they didn't consider it their job to act as his protector. Not like he did for them.

"I'm fine," he assured her, pulling her hands off his face. "Now, speaking of my family—" he began.

"We weren't. I asked a question and you lied." She narrowed her gaze and frowned at him, reinforcing how smart she was.

"So my segue sucked but I need to tell you something. They're arriving here. Soon."

Her eyes opened wide. "I'm sorry, what?" She raised her voice as obvious panic set in. "Your family, as in your stepmother, father, and all your siblings are coming *here*? To the island?"

He held back a chuckle at her reaction because it was a fair one, and she'd get pissed if he laughed.

"Okay," Nikki said, all but wringing her hands, the prospect of being surrounded by new people clearly sending her spiraling.

"Breathe." He grasped both her hands in his. "I was so caught up in everything going on with you, and between us, I forgot all about the planned weekend. And it's not everyone.

My stepmom and my dad are coming for their anniversary. Zach and Harrison decided to join them. Nobody else can make it."

Now that he thought about it, Harrison might have tried to remind him about the weekend when Asher had spoken to his brother from the airport. He'd been too stunned by the sight of Nikki to pay attention.

"Four people," she said, more to herself than him. "Your brothers and your parents. I think can handle that."

He nodded. "You can."

"I need to shower. Make myself presentable." She scrambled off the bed, pulling on the bottom half of her clothes. "Asher?"

"What is it?"

She looked up at him. "Do you think they know about the pictures? Will they judge me?" she asked, sounding as vulnerable as he'd ever seen her.

Everything in him softened at her fear of what his family would think of her, no doubt caused by how her parents blamed her instead of being on her side.

"No, honey, they won't. That's not who they are." He could easily make that promise.

"Okay, good." Her shoulders lowered and she nodded, her expression filled with relief. She turned and walked toward the door.

"Nikki."

She turned back to face him.

"Come find me when you're ready."

A grateful smile lit up her face before she walked out.

He drew a deep breath and ran a hand through his hair, wondering what the hell was happening between them and whether his brothers would notice and give him shit for it. In the way siblings always did.

He thought back to her question after he unloaded about his past. They both knew he'd lied to her. He wasn't always *fine* but he'd never thought about who looked out for him before. Not until that moment. Until she'd poked and prodded at vulnerabilities that forced him to admit, if only to himself, he wished she could be that person.

His person.

Considering the problems between them, her age and her brother's reaction to Asher sleeping with her, that was a wish he shouldn't be having. But he couldn't deny his growing feelings for Nikki. Couldn't discount the warmth in his chest when he looked at her or the way sliding inside her felt like coming home. She settled him in ways no one and nothing else did.

But it wasn't right. Derek trusted him to take care of her, not take her to bed. And she was so young. She'd barely lived a life or knew who she really was. He shouldn't be thinking about anything long-term. Besides, he was looking for trouble where there wasn't any. They were having an affair. One they shouldn't have started, but they both knew things would end when they returned home. He'd said as much and she'd agreed.

But his gut churned at the idea of letting her go.

★ ★ ★

NIKKI STEPPED OUT of the shower. She cracked the bathroom door, and while waiting for the mirror to clear, she lathered her body in her coconut-scented moisturizer. With the towel wrapped around her, she stared at her bare-faced reflection in the mirror. Here on the island, she'd been relaxed and very much herself, but now she had Asher's family coming. Should she dress up, as much as possible, given how little she'd brought with her? Or did she go natural and hope for the best?

All her life, makeup and clothing had been her cover. A façade that helped her face the world. She was well aware that need came from her mother's constant pushing. Most mothers would angst over the right time to allow their daughters to wear makeup to school. They didn't want them to grow up too soon. They worried what was age appropriate. Not Nikki's mother.

From the time Nikki turned eleven and hit her awkward stage, Collette did everything she could to make sure the normal teen things about Nikki didn't embarrass *her*. Cover-up for teenage breakouts quickly became foundation to hide other imperfections Nikki would never have noticed but her mother did.

Considering how badly her mother had nitpicked Nikki's looks, she'd never know how she'd found the courage to participate in pageants and modeling. Yet she had. But with her mother's words ringing in her ears, she'd rarely left the house without a full face of makeup.

Until she'd moved into her own place in New York City and escaped from her overbearing parents. Once alone, she'd come into herself. When not working, Nikki wore minimal makeup. Which was why she shouldn't change things up now, she decided. Asher promised his family wouldn't judge her and she had to believe him.

She dried her hair until it was damp and put it up in the messy bun she preferred in the island heat. Her face was tan from her days outside, and she swiped on waterproof mascara and shimmery peach lip gloss. She wore a floral summer dress and sandals. Collette would curl her lip at Nikki's casual, fun look, which only cemented the fact that she'd chosen correctly.

The moment she stopped considering what to wear, thoughts of her night with Asher came floating into her mind. He was everything she wanted for her future. A good, solid, trustworthy, man who accepted her for who she was, inside and out. It was ironic that once again, the love she wanted in her life, she couldn't have. He'd made that very clear. She had their time on the island. Nothing more.

Her stomach hurt at the truth but she was used to falling short. She'd never been enough for someone to love. Her parents, especially her mother, never had.

She shook her head to clear her thoughts. There would be other days in the future to daydream about her time in Asher's bed. How they'd trusted each other with stories of the past and shared their pain. Right now it was time meet his family and hopefully learn even more about the man she was falling for but couldn't keep.

Chapter Eight

WITHIN MINUTES OF meeting the Dares, Nikki adored Asher's parents and brothers. Their warmth and giving nature were obvious, making Nikki immediately wish she had a family that was as welcoming on sight. Or at all.

After the introductions, which consisted of, "This is Derek's sister, Nikki". Asher gave no explanation why she was here and nobody asked.

Serenity had stepped forward and pulled Nikki into an it's-so-good-to-meet-you hug, which Nikki returned, all the while making comparisons in her own life. Like when was the last time her mother had been affectionate toward her? The fact that she couldn't remember gave her the answer, and a painful knot had formed in her stomach.

After eating sandwiches Maggie had made, everyone dispersed to their rooms to unpack, changed into bathing suits, and met up at the pool. Nikki was already on a lounge chair with Lucky by her side. Maggie had put a doggie bowl of water by the house doors, and her smart boy had immediately learned to go there for a drink.

"Hey there, pretty girl." Asher's brother, Zach, sat down on the chair beside her. "How are you?"

Unlike Asher, who always had a more buttoned-up appearance, Zach had a bad-boy look to him, mostly thanks to the scruff on his jaw she sensed was more an everyday thing than him being lazy during vacation. His hair was on the longer side, appearing as if he ran his hands through it often, and though she had no idea, she would bet women loved the look.

She preferred Asher, her suit-wearing grump. Who she was learning wasn't such a grump the more she got to know him.

She lifted her sunglasses and perched them on her head to meet Zach's gaze. "I'm good. How was your flight?"

"No complaints since I slept through it." He stretched out his legs on the chair beside her.

She laughed. "I'm betting your family thought you were great company."

He grinned. "They had each other to talk to. I had a late night but I feel better now."

"Asher told me you own a bar? I imagine that would lead to long working hours."

He nodded, folding his hands behind his head. "And you would be right."

Lucky nudged his nose against Zach's leg, and he stretched out a hand to pet the pup's head. "He's yours?"

Nikki nodded. "I found him on the beach when we went jet skiing. He was a stray and I couldn't leave him behind." She watched as Zach continued to rub Lucky's head, the dog nuzzling his nose into Zach's thigh.

"I have to ask. How did you get Mr. Everything's Perfect to let you bring a dog home?" He tipped his head toward where Asher stood talking with his parents.

Harrison was at the far side of the pool, taking a phone call.

At Zach's description of his brother, Nikki laughed. "Truth? I smiled, begged, and opened the car door for the dog to jump in."

Zach stared in silence.

"What's wrong?"

"You've worked magic, that's all. Asher's pretty rigid in his life. You're good for him. I like it." Zach nodded in approval.

Nikki wondered how to interpret his words. "Asher is doing my brother a favor by letting me stay here and… we've become friends."

She did her best not to blush at the lie. If last night and this morning were anything to go by, she and Asher went beyond friends. Of course, just because they'd slept together didn't mean he wanted more, even if it felt like their connection ran deeper than a one-night stand.

"Friends," Zach said, glancing at Asher, whose gaze was steadily watching her. "If you say so."

Her face warmed and it wasn't from the sun. Before she could answer, Maggie walked over and handed out glasses of iced tea.

"Thank you," Nikki said, gratefully taking the drink.

"Zach? Do you want a drink?"

"No thanks. I have my beer." He held up a bottle. "I miss you, Maggie. Is my brother treating you right?" Zach asked with what Nikki figured other women would call a panty-dropping grin.

Maggie rolled her eyes. "That cheeky smile won't work on me, and yes, your brother is a wonderful employer. Now behave," she chided him. But she walked away laughing.

"I'm her favorite," Zach informed Nikki smugly.

She couldn't help the smile tugging at her mouth. This Dare brother was outgoing and fun.

"Now where were we?" Zach turned to face her. "Ahh. I remember what I wanted to say. You said you're here as a favor to your brother, and I was about to ask how you're *really* holding up?" He took a long sip of his beer.

Hers was cold in her hand.

"You know about me." She swallowed hard, doing her best not to show her embarrassment, assuming Zach had seen the pictures.

"I do. Thanks to Harrison's career, I tend to read the tabloid shit. You know, to look out for him."

So Asher wasn't the only Dare brother with the need to protect those he cared about. Michael and Serenity had raised good men.

"I also realize what happened was not your fault. Tell me what you're doing to figure out who set you up," Zach said.

"Are you harassing my girl – I mean are you bothering Nikki?" Asher stepped up to the end of her chair, blocking the sun.

Zach shook his head. "Nah. We're just getting to know each other."

The sound of her phone ringing saved her from having to deal with both of them at one time.

She glanced at the screen, seeing Meg's name flash. Huh. It was about time her *friend* called to check on her. She'd gotten texts from Winter after their last conversation, the other woman wanting to touch base and make sure Nikki was okay. Unlike Meg, Winter was warm and seemed genuine, making Nikki like her even more.

"Excuse me," Nikki said to the men, swinging her legs off the chair and walking a few steps away to take the call. She tapped the screen. "Hello?"

"Oh my God, Nikki. Where *are* you?" Meg asked. "Why haven't you called me and told me how you decided to handle your mess?"

Nikki rolled her eyes. In the short couple of days she'd been away, she'd seen the distinct difference between a friend – Winter – and a selfish narcissist – Meg. She hadn't even asked how Nikki was doing.

"Hello, Meg. I'm just taking some time to myself until things blow over."

"Well, you are missing out by not being here. With you MIA, guess who they gave your spot in the upcoming bridal show?"

Nikki waited for the jealousy to hit over the fact that she couldn't be there, but all she felt was betrayal at the glee in Meg's voice. Along with the rush of certainty that the modeling world and the people in it weren't for her.

"Well, it seems things worked out in your favor," Nikki said, her voice brittle.

"I agree. And it's about time, don't you think?" Meg asked.

Oh, here she goes. The poor-me routine, Nikki thought. "Look, you got what you wanted now that I'm not there to get in your way."

"Where are you, anyway, and when will you be back?" Meg asked.

Nikki looked out at the luxurious infinity pool, knowing she was lucky to have this hideaway. One she had no intention of sharing. "I'm with a friend."

"Male or female?"

"Meg, I'm busy right now. I'm not even interested in modeling anymore, so you don't have to worry about me as your *competition*." The words, once out, sounded perfect to her ears.

"And what is it that interests you instead?" Meg asked in a snarky tone.

Nikki glanced over at Harrison, who, along with his parents, had joined Zach and Asher by the lounge chairs. Nikki recalled her conversation with Winter about her interview with the actor and his production partners. "I don't know. Maybe I'll look into learning about making movies?"

Meg let out a bark of laughter. "Really? Because you have *so* much experience." She paused. "Then again, you had the connections to be successful in modeling. I'm sure whatever you want to do next will be no exception. So when *are* you coming back?"

"Meg?"

"Yes?"

"I need to go. And since you don't really like me, you should lose my number." Relief filling her, Nikki disconnected the call before Meg could utter another word.

She turned to find Asher had joined her. "Oh! Hi."

"Hi. Everything okay?" he asked.

She smiled wide. "Actually? Everything is great." All other things considered. And if she didn't somehow feel the eyes of everyone in his family on them, she'd kiss him with all the happiness she felt.

Because she'd dumped parts of her she hadn't realized were weighing her down so badly, from Meg to the career she didn't love. But mostly because this man had come into her life, and for whatever reason, his grumpy self made her happy.

★ ★ ★

NIKKI EXCUSED HERSELF to take a phone call, leaving Asher alone with Zach. Asher sat beside his brother and looked over, watching her expression as she spoke on the phone. Whoever called was upsetting her.

"Okay, spill." Zach smacked Asher on the shoulder.

"Nikki is here as a favor to her brother. My friend Derek. You've met him."

Zach inclined his head, his gaze never leaving Asher's. "I get it. Letting the girl with the naked photos hide out here is the favor. But that's not what I'm asking."

Asher raised an eyebrow. "You're going to have to

be more specific." No way was he giving away such personal information easily. Although knowing his intuitive brother, he'd already figured it out.

"You can't stop staring at her. How long was she here before you took her to bed?"

Asher stiffened. "None of your damned business."

At that, Zach burst out laughing. "Thanks for answering my question. She means something to you."

Asher merely shook his head. "It's not like that."

"Then tell me what it's like? You two keep making eyes at each other when you think no one's looking. But you're worried. That much is obvious. If I had to guess? I'd say you're concerned she's too young for you and you think Derek will kill you for touching his sister." Zach leaned back in the recliner and took a sip of the beer he'd brought over with him.

Asher curled one hand around the edge of the lounge. "I don't get it. You own a bar, you hack like a pro, and you're intuitive as fuck. What else *do* you do?" And why did nobody know for sure beyond the bar?

Zach lifted his shoulders. "I make use of the talents I have, bro."

That was the nonanswer Asher had expected.

"So I'm right?" Zach asked, pushing about Asher's feelings for Nikki.

"Let's say you are." Asher eyed his brother. "Given you are a single, woman-hopping bachelor, what advice do you have for me?" He gave his brother shit, but the truth was, Asher valued Zach's opinion and his sibling knew it. Ribbing and busting each other's balls was part of their lives.

Zach raised his hand to shield his eyes from the glare. Even with sunglasses, at this hour of the day, the sun hit at a tough angle. "Hmm. Knowing you, you wouldn't get involved with an airhead, and I've already spoken to her a bit so I know she's smart. And with her pedigree, she's probably wise for her age. As for worrying about Derek?" He waved his free hand. "Don't. You do you. See where this thing goes and deal with the fallout later."

Not a bad way of thinking about things, Asher mussed. It wasn't like he'd be able to keep his hands off Nikki anyway.

"Just be prepared for your friend to kick your ass before he comes around to the idea of you two as a couple," Zach added under his breath but loud enough to be heard.

"Fucking swell."

Zach laughed. "You have time to figure things out. Just be glad Nikki's been spared Jade and Aurora visiting."

Asher cringed at the thought. "They'd be great with her but–"

"They'd be all over your ass, cementing your future." Zach tilted the bottle and finished what was left of the beer, placing it on the table beside him.

"Hey. It's not like you're serious about anyone," Asher reminded him.

"And it'll stay that way. But the girls do want us to settle down," Zach muttered, inclining his head toward Harrison to include him in their sisters' hopes and dreams.

"And they tell us all the time," Asher agreed.

As often as all three claimed marriage wouldn't be happening for them any time soon, it didn't quite ring true. Wasn't that what Nick, the traveling bachelor with no home base, had said before finding Aurora and the child he'd never known about?

And hadn't Jade given up on relationships until Knox had battered down her walls, which had been higher than Asher's? With two broken engagements, she'd had good reason not to trust. Until she'd found the right man.

Which left him wondering. Despite his and Nikki's age difference and the fact that her brother would string him up by his balls, could Nikki be that right person for Asher? A warm feeling settled in his chest at the thought, both unnerving him and feeling too fucking good.

Before he could freak out, Serenity, his father, and Harrison walked over, joining them. Serenity was a beautiful woman. Her hair had been long until she'd recently had it cut to her shoulders, accentuating her features. Most importantly, she had a good heart.

"I'm so happy to be here," Michael said. "I wish everyone could have come but it's also nice to get more one-on-one time with you boys."

Boys. Asher held back a laugh, knowing what his father meant. "I'm happy you're here, too." He rose to his feet. "Serenity, take the chair."

"Thanks, hon." She treated him to a warm smile and sat down, stretching out her legs.

His father lowered himself on the end of her seat, placing a hand on his wife's calf. Harrison settled on the edge of Zach's chair, shoving his legs to the other side to give himself more room.

"I'll get more lounges in this area so we can all talk."

Asher pulled out his phone and texted Corey to rearrange the chairs, then glanced at his family. "I want to check on Nikki. I'll be right back."

He walked over where she was still on her call, facing away from him.

"Meg?" Nikki paused. "I need to go. And since you don't really like me, you should lose my number." She disconnected the call and turned around, noticing him for the first time. "Oh! Hi."

Her tone and cool words hadn't sounded like the

Nikki he knew. But if she was standing up for herself around the so-called friends she said she couldn't trust? He was all for it.

"Hi," he said. "Everything okay?"

Her smile filled him in places he hadn't known were empty.

"Actually? Everything is great." Her eyes sparkled with the truth of her statement.

"Okay then." He let out a relieved breath, glad she wasn't upset.

"I told Meg I'm finished with modeling, too."

He shook his head. "I should be surprised but you've said you aren't happy. Still, don't you want to think things through after all this… *other stuff* blows over?" He didn't mention the photos.

He'd been in touch with Derek, and the social media frenzy surrounding Nikki was dying down. The reporters weren't stalking her building anymore, which meant they were getting closer to the end. He knew Nikki had spoken to her brother, too, but she hadn't mentioned it and Asher didn't bring it up.

"No. I don't need to think. For the first time, I can see clearly. Even if I hate the reason I had to hide, getting away has helped me clear my mind." She shrugged, seeming calm. "I have to tell my agent, but I'm certain. I have enough in savings for me to take time off after I get home and figure out what comes next."

Zach was right. She was smart and wise for her age. Not that Asher hadn't noticed it before. "How about you come hang out with my family and later you can spend some time with Harrison and ask him about movie production?"

Nikki stared.

"What is it?" he asked.

"You get me." She'd said something similar last night, but now she sounded truly surprised. "Where my parents would be yelling, where Derek would support me but worry, you're just… there for me. Helping me move forward."

"You're bright, Nikki. You're smart enough to know what you want. I believe in you."

Her eyes filled and she flung herself at him, wrapping her arms around his neck. "Thank you."

He hugged her back, ignoring the heat of her against his bare chest and trying not to imagine what his family was thinking about them as he held on tight.

★ ★ ★

LATER THAT NIGHT, after a surprise lobster dinner that Maggie had arranged, Asher sat in the comfortably large family room with his parents and Zach, having an after-dinner drink. It was late and everyone was tired after their day of travel and time out in the sun. The men wore shorts and the women were in light dresses, the typical casual outfits when on the island.

Serenity had just finished telling a story about how the boys had gotten themselves into trouble in college. "Nothing too serious, thank goodness."

"I'm already turning gray," Michael said. "I definitely am ready for a little peace and quiet, which I thought I would get once they were away." He chuckled and shook his head. "It's a wonder we survived all of you."

Asher grinned.

"Amen," Zach added.

"What are Harrison and Nikki talking about? They've been huddled together for an hour," Zach said.

Asher glanced at the two sitting in the far corner of the room. "I'm pretty sure he's telling her about filmmaking and production. She's had it with modeling and wants to quit for good."

"That poor girl." Serenity's expression softened. "She's been through a lot, having to hide out until the press leaves her alone."

"She has no parental support, either." He wasn't betraying Nikki's confidence, as Derek had always told him as much.

"You know, I've seen her mother at a luncheon to

raise money for pancreatic cancer. We didn't meet face to face but the aura she gives off is a cold one." Serenity shook her head. "Nikki deserves people who have her best interests at heart, and it was obvious Collette Bettencourt cared only about her husband's political life and his becoming president one day."

As someone who'd raised five kids in addition to her own four, Serenity wouldn't understand an aloof woman like Nikki's mother. "At least she has her brother," Asher said.

"Who would do something like that to her?" Michael asked, without mentioning the specifics.

Asher frowned. "Derek is supposed to be questioning people in her life and talking to a private investigator."

Zach cleared his throat and Asher glanced over. "Yeah, I'll get you on the phone with him first thing in the morning," he said, reading his brother's mind. Zach had connections. When Jade's ex-fiancé had lost his mind and kidnapped her, it had been Zach who'd found her and led the charge to get her back.

Satisfied, Zach leaned back in his seat, his gaze going to where Harrison's and Jade's heads were close together. "Are you sure they're talking about work?"

"Jesus," Asher muttered, despite knowing Zach was just being his irrepressible self.

"I can't believe I have to say this at your age, but

leave your brother alone, Zachary." Serenity shook her head at him, but her lips pursed in an attempt to withhold a laugh.

A cold nose nudged at Asher's calf, and he glanced down to see Lucky rubbing against Asher's bare leg. He absently scratched at the dog's head.

"He's such a sweet thing," Serenity said. "I'm surprised you let him in, dog hair and all." They all knew he'd never been interested in a pet and preferred things neat and in their places.

Asher opened his mouth to answer but Zach beat him to it. "He couldn't say no to Nikki."

"Pretty much." Why deny it?

"I like her," Michael said. "But isn't she a little young for you?"

Serenity immediately nudged her husband in the side while Asher let out a disbelieving laugh. "Even if that is true" ¬¬—and his father *had* hit a nerve – "wouldn't you call it hypocritical to call me out on it? After all, I'm the one who remembers the kids making fun of me in school because they thought my father was fucking the nanny–" He cut himself off with a growl. "Shit, Serenity. I'm sorry. That was uncalled for."

"It's okay," she said quietly, but the hurt was there, the damage done.

"No, it's not. I *am* sorry." He was usually a lot better at keeping his feelings beneath his shields.

Apparently, his talks with Nikki about how it had felt growing up had brought the pain to the surface and it'd bubbled out. But his father shouldn't have said what he had and Asher shot him a knowing glare.

Michael dipped his head, accepting responsibility. He wasn't yelling at Asher for his hurtful words because Asher had already apologized to his stepmother.

Nikki's squeal interrupted the awkwardness that had settled between them. She rose and pumped Harrison's hand until he calmed her down with a pat on the back as he led her over to the rest of the family.

Asher rose to his feet, grateful for something else to focus on. He felt like a big enough ass without time to dwell on it in uncomfortable silence.

"Harrison offered me the chance to intern at his company! He said he'd talk to Sasha, Cassidy, and Xander. I can decide if I want to learn the developmental side, reading scripts and things or production, like being on set."

"Either way, a production assistant is a lot of gopher work," Harrison warned her.

"I'm okay with that!"

Glancing at his sibling, Asher treated him to a grateful nod. "Congratulations," he told her, trying to imbue excitement in his tone.

"Hey, she's eager to learn, and I know for sure Sasha and Cassidy would be happy to have her on board. Don't worry. We'll find the perfect spot for her."

Beside him, Nikki was nearly bouncing with exhilaration, and Asher was thrilled for her. But Harrison, astute as ever, glanced at everyone and narrowed his gaze. "What's going on?"

"Everyone's tired," Michael said, rising and pulling Serenity with him. "I think we all just need a good night's sleep."

Asher took the cue. "I agree. If anyone needs anything, just shoot me a text and I'll get it taken care of."

Zach stood. "I know how to raid the fridge. It'll be fine." He turned to Nikki, who now seemed subdued, no bouncing in excitement, her gaze darting between everyone, trying to figure things out. "Congratulations, pretty girl. Harrison and his partners will take good care of you." Zach winked at her. "Night, all."

"I'll turn in, too," Harrison said.

They walked off, heading for the stairs.

"I think that's our cue," Michael said. "We'll talk in the morning, son," he said, his gaze on Asher.

Asher nodded back, the lump in his throat huge. "Serenity, I'm really–"

She touched his shoulder. "It's fine. *We're* fine."

Michael took her hand and led her in the direction

the others had gone.

Asher shook his head. Jesus. How the hell had that come out of his mouth? He heard their footsteps on the stairs.

Obviously so did Nikki as she turned to him, confusion in her eyes. "What did I interrupt?"

He let out a groan, knowing he had no choice but to explain. The truth would hurt her feelings, but it wasn't like she didn't already know he thought their age difference was an issue.

He reached for her hand and she placed her palm in his. "Come on. I'll explain."

Chapter Nine

NIKKI DIDN'T LIKE the look on Asher's face or the sudden change in atmosphere. Something she'd noticed when she'd squashed her excitement over Harrison's offer long enough to pay attention. This family was close. The chill in the room told her something had shaken them.

Nikki glanced at Lucky and patted her thigh. The dog rose to his feet and followed her as Asher led her to his room. Curiosity warred with concern.

He shut and locked the doors behind them. "Why don't you sit?" He gestured to the bed and she hopped on, wanting answers. Lucky took that as an invitation and jumped up beside her. He walked to the edge of the mattress, stretched out, and watched the humans.

Asher didn't say a word about the dog on his bed. That, along with the cloudiness in his eyes, had her stomach churning. "What's going on?" she asked.

"Everything was fine. We were sitting around and talking, and my father said he liked you."

She tilted her head, confused. "That's a good thing, yes?"

Asher nodded. "It should have been but that

wasn't all he said."

Her stomach twisted into a knot, and she drew her knees to her chest. "Was it the photos? Am I too much of an embarrassment?"

"No! That wasn't it." Asher stepped over and settled on the other side of the bed, causing the mattress to dip beside her. "He said he liked you but he also asked if you were too young for me."

She swallowed hard. "I see." So his father had reinforced an issue Asher already had about them. "And you agreed?" Her fingers curled into the material of the comforter, waiting for his reply.

Asher's tension didn't help. His jaw was tight, a muscle twitching there. "Actually, I snapped back that it was a hypocritical thing for him to say… considering I was the one who remembered the kids in school making fun of me because my father was fucking the nanny."

"Oh God." Nikki slapped a palm over her open mouth.

Asher dipped his head and groaned. "I know. Believe me, I know. It was a shitty thing to say." He glanced up, a flush covering his cheekbones. "The words just came out, and I apologized to Serenity immediately."

Nikki touched his shoulder. Not knowing what to say, she waited for him to go on.

"It's just, you and I had been talking, and we'd admitted a lot of painful things. I think the suppressed hurt I'd never dealt with was waiting at the surface, ready to be triggered. And my father's question did it."

She blew out a long breath, gathering her thoughts. Her goal was to help him, not make him feel worse. "That makes sense and I'm sure it'll all get smoothed over." Serenity had already reassured him, and his father had said they'd talk tomorrow. "Are you okay?" Nikki asked.

He lifted his shoulders in a slight shrug. "I'm sure it'll blow over like you said. I'll be fine."

Which brought them to the bigger issue for them. "Is my age still a problem for you?" She waited, praying for him to contradict her.

How could she hope for a chance in the future if he was still stuck on that point? And she needed that hope no matter what she'd verbally agreed to.

He closed his eyes for a brief moment, long enough to answer the question.

She turned to leave, sliding her legs off her side of the bed, but he grasped her wrist, stopping her. "Don't go."

She didn't spin back to face him. Heart in her throat, she waited to hear what he had to say.

"There are different ways to look at it," he said in a gruff voice. "On the one hand, you're smart and know your own mind. On the other, at twenty-one, you've just begun to explore who you are, and I don't want to get in the way of you being able to do that. God knows I'm not the same person I was at your age."

At least he was thoughtful about the facts. And he'd acknowledged she could make her own choices.

She turned and resettled herself on the bed, crossing her legs beneath her. Meeting his gaze, she asked, "How many twenty-one-year-olds do you know that have traveled the world? Modeled in New York, Paris, London, and Milan? Met the DC elite, the current president, and is the daughter of a potential future leader of the Free World?"

A grudging smile of admiration lifted his sexy lips. "So what I'm hearing is you're not *most* women."

The teasing note in his voice released the knot that had formed in her chest, and she shook her head. "I never have been."

"Nikki…" He stroked a hand down her cheek, a touch she felt deep inside. "I already told you I can't make promises…"

"And I'm not asking for any." Even if she wanted them, she knew better than to demand one. Her relationship with Asher was as fluid as the enigmatic man himself.

Not finished touching her, he tucked a strand of hair behind her ear. "I also can't claim to know what the future holds."

"I never said you were a fortune teller, Asher. I agreed to time on the island only. I'm just saying to open your mind while we're together. Your father made his point, and after that comparison you made, he's not going to give you a hard time again. Pot, kettle, and all that."

He let out a wry laugh. "True."

"I like your family and you said they like me. We're not shoving our relationship in their faces, and we aren't exactly putting on a PDA show. They won't even know what we are to each other while they're here. They might guess but that's all it will be." She held her breath, hoping he'd agree.

"They saw you hugging me by the pool," he told her, his lips twitching. "Zach's got us all figured out, and if my father felt the need to mention the age gap, so has he."

She lifted her shoulders. "So? Are they going to gossip to my brother?" Because that was Asher's other main worry. Letting down the good friend who'd trusted him.

Nikki could handle Derek, but until there was a reason to tell him, she'd rather cement her relationship with Asher first. That would give Asher a reason to fight for her rather than let her go. That was her ultimate goal, even if he didn't know it yet. But the decision was his. She couldn't force him to want to be with her in the future.

"They won't talk about us to anyone," he said, sounding certain.

"Then we don't have anything to worry about." And she intended to make him forget anything that still lingered in his mind, upsetting him. "Talk time is over."

Scooting closer, she reached for the hem of his shirt and lifted it over his head. With his help, she pulled off his top and tossed the garment to the floor. She rose to her knees and pushed him back against the pillows.

No sooner had she moved than the dog rose to his feet.

Asher glanced over. "Lucky, bed." He gestured to the fuzzy dog bed she hadn't noticed in the corner.

She blinked in surprise. "When did you get that?" she asked, looking from the floor to Asher.

He shrugged. "I asked Corey to pick one up today," he said, as if it were no big deal.

But it was. It really was.

Too bad Lucky didn't understand.

With a groan, Asher pushed himself off the bed and whistled for the dog. Lucky hopped off and Asher, in his commanding alpha mode, pointed at the spot he wanted him. "Come on. Go."

With a reluctant whine, the dog slowly made his way over and lay down, looking sad and put out.

Nikki smiled. "I wonder if someone owned him before he ended up as a stray. He's so good."

"Probably. I can't say I'm thrilled with him watching us," Asher muttered, climbing back onto the bed and stretching out the way he'd been before.

She held back a laugh at the comment, and instead of focusing on her pet, she crawled back to Asher, picking up where she'd left off.

She worked open the button of his shorts and lowered the zipper over the bulge of his erection. He lifted his hips, sliding his shorts and boxer briefs down his legs. He kicked them off and sprawled back against the pillows, eyes glazed with desire.

Though she felt the pulse deep in her sex, she ignored her own needs. She had Asher naked, spread out for her, and she took advantage. She started at his lips, kissing him deep, showing him what was building in her heart. She took her time, enjoying the way his hand came up to cup her head, grip her hair, and tug on the long strands.

Desire pulsed between her thighs, and she let out a moan but she was determined not to let him take over. She slid her mouth downward, licking the warm skin at his neck, inhaling his masculine musky scent, and sucking along his collarbone.

His hips bucked and he attempted to roll her over, but she held him down by his shoulders. "I want to do this." She met his gaze, willing him to understand. "I need to be in control."

To show him what she could give to him. That this relationship wasn't one-sided. She wasn't just here to hide away from the world, to take his help and support, and to sneak into his bed at night. She needed him to see her as someone capable of giving back when he needed her. Though she was young, she could be his partner if he'd let her. She'd already proven she could listen and give him advice. Now she wanted to show she could soothe him in other ways, too.

She caught the easing of his expression, and his muscles released beneath her touch. He was giving her what *she* needed. Now she could return the favor.

She spread her hands over his chest, brushing her thumbs over his nipples, and he released a rumbling groan.

"If you were naked, I'd be having an even harder time not grabbing your wrists and holding them over your head so I could lick your nipples and work on making you come."

Her sex squeezed at his explicit words. "Which is why I'm not naked yet." She inched her way down his body until she was beside his hip. Reaching over, she wrapped her fingers around his cock and pumped her hand a couple of times, causing a white pool of pre-come to settle on top.

She dipped her head and sucked him deep. Despite her claim of wanting control, when he pumped his hips up and down, setting his own rhythm, she allowed him to take what he needed. He continued to thrust upward until her jaw ached and her hand grew damp from working his cock along with her mouth. Without warning, he bucked up and lifted her off him.

She blinked in surprise. "What?"

"I need to be inside you. Now." Asher rolled to the side, opening the nightstand drawer.

She took the hint and climbed off the bed, quickly undressing, then dropping her clothes and panties on the floor before joining him again.

Next thing she knew, he had her flat on the bed, arms above her head, his big hand grasping her wrists. Just like he'd promised earlier.

She stared into his deep blue eyes as he positioned himself over her and, without waiting, thrust deep. Unlike their first time, Asher wasn't slow and gentle. The first time together they'd connected on a deep level and now was no different. As if he'd already learned her body, each time he tunneled deep, he took her higher, keeping up a fast rhythm, bringing her close to climax.

"God, Asher. I'm so close." She tried to move her arms, to touch his sweat-slickened skin, but he held on tight.

Instead of maintaining the hard and fast pace, he slowed down, sliding in and out more slowly. His gaze caught hers, watching each time he slid out and drove back in. The change in speed should have thrown her off, stopped the growing need to come.

But he'd shifted his hips, hitting her in a new spot, *the* spot. *His spot.* Once, twice, and she let go, seeing stars as a long, languid climax consumed her. It was perfect. *He* was perfect. She felt suspended for a long time, her body quaking as he found his own release.

With a groan, he collapsed on top of her, quickly shifting to his elbows and taking his weight off her so she could catch her breath. But their bodies were still connected until he held the edge of the condom and pulled out. The loss she felt was profound as he rose and walked to the bathroom.

When he returned, he climbed back onto the bed and wrapped himself around her once more. Now she felt complete. A shiver of panic followed the thought. She already knew he owned her body. Now she understood. He also owned her soul.

Time passed in sweet, comfortable silence that she didn't feel compelled to fill with her normal chatter.

Later, before falling asleep, Asher asked her about

her talk with Harrison. "I take it everything went well?" His fingers tangled in her hair, the tugging feeling good.

She nodded. "Your brother is a great guy. Look at the favor he's doing for me. Did you know he's being interviewed by my journalist neighbor? Her name is Winter Capwell and she's writing about the female-centric focus of his production company and talking to all the partners."

"I'm proud of how well their company is doing. Golden Globe and Academy Awards. They deserve the recognition," Asher said. "He mentioned the interview. I just didn't realize you knew the woman who's writing the piece."

Nikki shrugged. "I don't know her well. She's been nice to me and has checked on me throughout this mess."

Asher propped himself on one arm. "She's a reporter and she hasn't pressured you for your story or any information about where you are?"

"No, she hasn't. That's why I want to get to know her better. To see if she's someone I can be friends with. I don't have many of those," she reminded him.

He relaxed again and she lay in the crook of his arm. "In this new job, I'm sure you'll meet people who like you for the amazing woman you are."

She smiled at his praise. "Has Harrison mentioned

what he thinks about Winter?" Because he'd asked Nikki a lot of questions about the reporter.

"He said she's gorgeous. That's about it."

Nikki wrinkled her nose. "Her looks? That's all he's said about her?"

Asher let out a laugh. "Harrison's a player. That's what he notices first. One day he'll wake up and realize there's someone with depth he can be interested in for more than a quick one-night stand."

Their conversation drifted off and Nikki lay breathing in Asher's scent and appreciating the security of lying in his arms.

★ ★ ★

NIKKI MUST HAVE fallen asleep because next thing she knew, sunlight was streaming through the windows in Asher's bedroom. He was still out, his big body wrapped around hers, his breathing even. Another night of sleep. She might even set a record for herself of consecutive nights… as long as she was in Asher's bed.

Nope. She couldn't think about that. Instead, she glanced at the small digital clock on the nightstand. Six a.m. She didn't want Asher's parents to realize she'd slept in his room. Hopefully, she could sneak upstairs before Michael or Serenity saw her coming out of here. Though they were adults, she'd still be embarrassed if she ran into them.

A small snore escaped from Asher, and she held back a laugh as she slipped out of his bed. She gathered her clothes and pulled on her undergarments. One of Asher's button-downs lay on a chair in the corner. At this point she wasn't sure what was worse. Her dress from last night or Asher's shirt.

Since her dress looked horribly wrinkled, she chose Asher's shirt. In the bathroom, she splashed her face and fixed her hair as best she could before tipping her head at the dog, who hopped off and followed her out.

Nikki already heard the sounds of Maggie humming in the kitchen, and Lucky headed in that direction. Knowing the sweet woman would let the dog out and feed him, Nikki turned toward the stairs.

The walk to her room felt like it took longer than usual, but she didn't run into anyone until she reached her door.

Just as Zach stepped out of his room.

"Hello there," he said, wearing a pair of shorts and a tee shirt, his hair still mussed from sleep.

"Hi." She braced herself for a comment about her sneaking into her room this morning, but he merely smiled.

"I'm going to get some coffee. Can I bring a cup back for you?" he asked.

She nodded. "That would be great. I'm going to jump in the shower, so would you leave it outside the door and I'll grab it?"

"Will do. And one more thing," Zach said.

"Yes?" she asked warily.

"I was hoping you, Asher, and I could talk later?" he asked.

She tilted her head to the side. "About?"

"Your… situation," he said delicately. "Let's just say I have skills, and I'd like to help you find out who posted the pictures."

She felt a blush rise to her cheeks, but she managed to laugh at his wording. "Yes, I've heard you have expertise in many things beyond owning a bar. And I'd appreciate the help."

"Sure thing, pretty girl." He winked at her. "See you at breakfast," he said and headed downstairs whistling.

She stepped into her room, shut the door, and leaned back against it. Zach, a stranger, wanted to help her.

In her world, well, that of her parents, help and aid were words used in campaign ads. In reality, they did what was best for themselves. She had no idea how Derek had become his own man, but thank goodness he had. Because Nikki had modeled herself after the brother she admired. No pun intended.

If Zach was willing to help with her problem, she would gratefully take him up on the offer.

★ ★ ★

ASHER WOKE UP alone, immediately realizing Nikki had snuck out early and why. He refused to think about how much he liked having her in his bed. Instead, he got up, took a long, hot shower, and dressed for the day. He was about to head to the kitchen to meet his parents for breakfast when his cell rang.

Derek's name flashed on the screen.

Asher took the call, and by the time he hung up, his stomach was churning and he didn't want to eat. Still, he joined everyone and drank coffee, knowing he was going to need the caffeine. Nikki was sitting with Serenity, talking, laughing, and enjoying her food.

He stood beside Zach at the island in the kitchen. "Hey. Sleep well?" Asher asked his brother.

Zach took a long sip of his coffee. "I think I should be asking you that question." He spoke low. "I saw your girl sneaking into her room this morning, wearing your shirt."

Asher raised his cup to his lips. He wouldn't dignify his brother's prying with an answer.

Zach swallowed and smirked. "I already told you I

like her, which is why I offered my assistance with her… photo problem."

Asher nodded, grateful. "I was going to talk to you about her situation regardless. I spoke to her brother, Derek, this morning, and he found a hidden camera in her bedroom," Asher said quietly so as not to be overheard.

Zach frowned, his protective instincts as strong as Asher's for people he cared about. "Text Derek. Set up a FaceTime or Zoom chat after the parents go into town." He tipped his head toward their father and Serenity. "Dad said Corey's taking them in a few."

Although Asher didn't want to put Nikki through the conversation, they had no choice.

He rose and walked over to the main table just as Michael and Serenity stood to leave. "We won't be back late," he said.

"Dad–" Asher began.

His father shook his head. "We're fine. She's fine. I still want to talk to you but it can wait. We're going to enjoy our day."

Serenity walked to Asher and pulled him into a hug.

He hugged her back. "I guess there were things I didn't deal with as well as I thought," he whispered. "Are we really good?"

She stepped back and patted his cheek. "Always."

Michael grasped her hand and they left for the day.

Asher let out a long breath, aware everyone had been watching.

"Nikki, you up for a chat with your brother, me, and Asher?" Zach asked, breaking into the silence.

"I'd like to sit in, too," Harrison said. "I hate what happened to you. Maybe I can help?"

Nikki wrapped her arms around herself and nodded. "I appreciate it."

Asher walked over and slid an arm around her. "It'll be okay."

She nodded.

A little while later, coffees refilled courtesy of Maggie, they gathered in Asher's study, with Derek pulled up on the computer screen.

Asher sat at a distance from Nikki, giving Derek the impression he was the same dick he'd always been. Present because Derek had asked and not because he was now personally invested.

Nikki twisted her fingers together in her lap, nerves written all over her, evidenced by her furrowed brows and tense expression. Asher had no doubt she hated having to discuss the situation at all. A room full of men only made it worse. But everyone here had her best interest at heart.

He shot her an understanding look, but that was all he could do with her brother basically in the room with them. Asher wanted to be beside her, holding her when they broke the bad news. Would it be that horrible for Derek to find out Asher and Nikki were together? Since it meant Asher, at thirty-three, hadn't been able to keep his hands off Derek's twenty-one-year-old sister? Yeah. It'd be bad.

"Nikki? Are you ready to talk?" Derek's voice broke into Asher's morose thoughts.

Nikki nodded. "I am. So what's going on at home?" She leaned forward for a better look at her brother, who glanced at Asher – because Derek had already told Asher about the camera.

Shit. Did Derek think his sister couldn't read a room?

Asher merely shook his head.

Nikki, meanwhile, stiffened and narrowed her eyes, her gaze darting between them. "What's going on? What do you two know that I don't?"

Asher decided the answer had to come from him. "Derek told me something this morning, and I didn't want to announce it at breakfast."

"Told you what?"

He met and held her stare, knowing there was no way to break the news easily. "Derek found a tiny hidden camera in your apartment. Your bedroom, to be exact."

"What?" she shrieked before breathing in and out,

obviously attempting to calm down. "Okay, okay," she said, more to herself than them. "I mean a camera makes sense, right? How else could someone have taken those photos?"

Derek ran a hand over his face and groaned. "I'm sorry, Nik. I hired someone to come in and do a sweep. They found it and asked if I wanted it removed."

"Of course I do!" Her voice rose again. She glanced at her trembling hands and shoved them beneath her thighs.

His brothers remained silent, obviously realizing this wasn't the time to interrupt, but Asher had had enough of Nikki's suffering.

He rose from his seat and sat down beside her. Without hesitating, he wrapped an arm around her waist, pulling her close. Whatever Derek took from his actions, Asher would deal with his friend later.

She put her head on his shoulder with a grateful sigh.

"You can't remove the camera," Zach said. Coffee in hand, he strode over and sat down on Nikki's other side. "I know this is scary as fuck, but what if the person who planted the camera plans to come back to get it?"

"How would they get in?" Harrison asked, speaking up for the first time.

"Same way they did the first time." Zach put a hand on her knee, and despite Asher knowing it was a gesture of comfort, he wanted to smack his brother's hand off her body. Irrational maybe but true. "Have you had anyone in lately to do work? Any delivery people who came into your bedroom?" Zach was in work mode.

She shook her head. "No. Definitely not."

"How about maintenance? Do they have a key?" Zach asked, removing his hand from her leg as he began to pace around the room, taking on the frenetic energy he got when he was working on something that intrigued him.

"No," Derek said. "My parents were adamant if she was going to live alone, nobody could have access."

"And what the senator wants, the senator gets," Nikki muttered.

Zach ran a hand through his hair. "Okay, then. Does someone have your key? You know, like a friend or a neighbor in case of emergencies?"

Asher schooled his features, but he knew that question had to have hit a nerve. He and Nikki had talked about her lack of close friends and how much it bothered her. Asher squeezed her shoulder in support. So far, Derek hadn't seemed to notice their connection.

"Only Derek has a key." She glanced at the screen and forced a smile for her brother's sake.

"Hmm." Zach paused by the floor-to-ceiling bookshelf, deep in thought.

"Oh, wait!" Nikki exclaimed and all eyes turned her way. "I lost my keys at a fashion shoot this past winter."

"Where?" Zach asked.

She named the studio. "In Lower Manhattan. I remember being panicked because I thought they were gone for good and I'd have to have the locks changed, but they turned up in my bag. It was weird because I'd emptied the whole thing out earlier."

Asher tapped her leg and she glanced up at him. "Could someone have taken them and put them back?" he asked though he knew the answer. He also had a gut feeling about who'd done it.

"I suppose. It's crazy busy behind the scenes of a show. Things are left everywhere," she murmured. "But who would…" She narrowed her gaze. "You have an idea, don't you?"

He nodded, and from the distraught look on her face, so did she.

"Meg?" she asked, sounding horrified.

Asher turned to meet Derek's gaze and lifted an eyebrow.

After the phone call Asher had overheard between

the women and how Nikki had cut the other model out of her life? That was exactly what he thought.

Derek sighed. “We don’t know for sure, and we can’t just accuse someone without proof. But I’ll get the locks changed.”

“Again, don’t.” Zach drummed his fingers on the bookshelf. “I want to see if someone comes back for the camera.”

“How? It’s a doorman building. How could someone get upstairs even with the keys?” Harrison asked.

Zach walked over to Harrison, and gave him a smack on the head. “How are we even related?” he muttered. “I mean don’t you actor types watch basic cop shows on TV?”

“Hey!” Harrison stood and elbowed his brother in the ribs.

Asher clapped his hands. Loudly. “Boys! Behave. And focus.”

Zach chuckled. “Right. Well, getting back to business, where there’s a will, there’s a way,” he said of how someone had entered the building. “Doormen take bathroom breaks. People join a group and walk in along with them. It happens.”

Harrison shrugged. “Excuse me for not being a super-spy,” he muttered.

“Okay. I’m going to need the full name of your friend along with any other suspicious people in your life," Zach said to Nikki. "That includes men you've flirted with, dated, or slept with," he matter-of-factly stated.

Nikki's eyes opened wide and she rose to her feet. "Umm… Derek can get you started with that information," she said, voice quivering. "I'll fill in the… umm… more personal stuff later. I'm going to get a drink from the kitchen," she said and rushed from the room.

"Is she okay?" Derek asked, sounding worried.

Asher curled his hands into fists, wanting, *needing* to go after her. But he had to play it cool in front of her brother, so he just nodded. "I think the camera thing upset her. She'll be fine."

"Yeah. I know she's in good hands with you," Derek said to Asher, who did his best not to wince.

"Text me Zach's cell and I'll send the information ASAP." Derek had already begun typing on his computer.

Pulling out his phone, Asher did as his friend asked, eager to end this conversation and go find Nikki.

"Why don't I go check on her?" Zach suggested.

"Good idea," Asher said to his sibling.

Zach strode to the door, and once he was out of Derek's view, he nodded at Asher. His version of, *I've got her.* His brother was covering his ass and Asher owed him one.

"Thanks, guys," Derek said. "I'm going to hang up and get to work on this list. Let's touch base again soon."

Derek disappeared from the screen, leaving Asher and Harrison alone in the study.

Asher glanced at his brother. "I need to go find Nikki, but I have a quick question for you first."

"Shoot," Harrison said.

"How do you know Nikki lives in a doorman building? Does it have something to do with a certain reporter?" Asher raised an eyebrow.

Harrison treated him to his movie-worthy smile. "What can I say? We hit it off."

"Your usual MO?" Meaning one night, maybe two, agreed upon upfront, no strings, no future.

Harrison didn't meet his gaze.

"What is it?" Asher asked.

"It's gone on a little longer than usual. But when the interviewing is finished, we're over."

Asher ran a hand through his hair. "Jesus. Nikki likes this woman, so do you think you can *not* be a dick when it ends?" In case Asher was lucky enough to get more time with Nikki off the island, her one potential friend wouldn't hate him because he was related to Harrison.

"That's insulting. I'm never a dick to women."

Harrison actually looked hurt. "But I'll make an extra effort with Winter. Now go find your girl and quit worrying about mine. I mean about me and my no-relationship motto."

Shaking his head, Asher left the room and walked through the house, looking for Nikki.

Chapter Ten

NIKKI WALKED DOWN to the beach with Lucky trotting along beside her. She trusted him to stick close. In a couple of days, he already knew where his food and affection came from. Zach had joined her in the kitchen and tried to cheer her up. Though she appreciated the effort, not even him calling her *pretty girl* in the fun way he had could get her to smile. Then he'd resorted to giving her his thoughts on the situation.

Lucky ran to the water and ducked and played in the shallow waves, getting wet sand on his paws. Nikki hoped she could sneak him to the tub before Maggie saw him and insisted on taking over. She didn't want to make more work for the kind woman. She had enough company to handle without adding Nikki's dirty dog to her to-do list.

"I looked all over the house for you." She heard Asher's voice before he sat down by her side.

"I needed air." She'd wrapped her arms around her knees and continued to stare out at the water.

Asher brushed her hair off her shoulders, his fingers grazing the sensitive skin of her neck, causing her to shiver despite the heat of the sun. "Looking for answers out there?"

She nodded. "The camera shouldn't have come as a surprise. How else could someone have taken naked photos of me?" She felt so violated she hadn't slept naked since unless she was secure in Asher's bedroom and in his arms.

"I guess I was in denial, because Derek's words took me off guard." She sighed, knowing that wasn't what bothered her most. She'd already come to terms with the pictures being out there. As much as she could, anyway.

He let out a harsh laugh. "Sometimes denial isn't a bad thing. And sometimes it comes back to bite you in the ass," he muttered.

She shook her head. "You haven't spoken to your father alone yet, have you?"

"No, but I will. Let's not change the subject. What's bothering you most?"

The answer came easily. "Could Meg really hate me so much she'd want to humiliate me in front of the entire world?" Her voice broke on the last word. She didn't want to think someone she'd spent so much time with, whether she liked Meg or not, could be that awful to her.

"C'mere." He pulled her to him and settled her in his lap.

Though she felt his hard erection beneath her, she didn't do anything but seek the comfort he'd offered. Wrapping her arms around his neck, she buried her face against his cheek and shoulder.

"To be honest? From the one-sided conversation I overheard yesterday, I'd say Meg is completely capable of hurting you, and you think so, too."

She nodded in agreement. Refusing to release him, she ignored the heat that had her dress plastered to her skin and his shirt covered in sweat. Instead, she focused on how their bodies connected and drew strength from him.

She took Asher's words about Meg seriously and thought about the woman and the often cold look in her eyes, and Nikki knew. "You're right. Meg probably took my keys."

"Was she around the day they went missing or did she disappear at some point?" he asked.

Nikki thought back. "Well, it's hard to say. We were all together for the show. Hair, makeup, it was crowded. But I don't recall her slipping away."

"So it's possible she took the keys, handed them to someone who had them copied and returned them," Asher said.

Nikki pulled out of his embrace and leaned back, meeting his gaze. "So you think she had an accomplice?"

"I've never met her, but I don't think she's smart enough to do it alone. Someone so consumed with hatred that *you'd* cut ties would be blinded by jealousy. They'd need help to pull off getting into your apartment, hiding a camera, and leaving again," he said.

"Now you sound like Zach." She glanced over her shoulder, checking on Lucky, who was still in the water, before turning back to Asher.

"We Dare men think alike, but in this case, I'll admit we talked before I came to find you. Those are his theories."

"He gave me that impression, too." With a lot fewer words.

Asher slid a hand behind her head and pulled her closer. "Stop thinking so hard. Zach will get a handle on the situation. In the meantime, you need other things to focus on." He dipped his head closer and sealed his lips over hers.

She kissed him back, enjoying the warmth of his kiss, the sensations he effortlessly pulled from her body. He shifted until he was on his knees and pushed her back into the sand and an uncontrollable laugh escaped.

"That's not the reaction I was looking for." His eyes twinkled like dark gems.

"I was thinking how hard it was going to be to get the sand out of my hair."

He smoothed a hand over her cheek, brushing the long strands off her face. "Something else is extremely hard," he said, rubbing his thick erection against her lower belly.

Sensations raced over her and she moaned, arching her hips to grind against him. Suddenly a spray of water hit them, soaking Asher most because he was on top.

"Shit!" He rolled off her, and she sat up to find Lucky shaking his body, water flying off his fur.

Nikki laughed, something finally breaking the wall of depression that had surrounded her since hearing from Derek. "Lucky, cut that out!"

"Cock blocker," Asher muttered. He rose to his feet, extending a hand toward Nikki.

She placed her palm in his and let him pull her up.

"Come on. Looks like we all need a shower." Asher glared at the pup, but she caught the hint of a smile lifting his lips.

The dog had grown on him and she loved it.

"The mutt is going with Maggie, and *you* are coming with me so we can finish what we started," Asher said as they trudged to the house in their sand-covered clothes.

A shiver of anticipation slid through her, and she decided she'd let Maggie bathe the dog one more time and make it up to her later.

★ ★ ★

THE STRESS OF the morning had gotten to Nikki, and after their shared shower, she crawled into Asher's bed and fell into a deep sleep. Although she said she had trouble sleeping, being in his bed obviously soothed her.

He left her there and spent the day with his brothers, something they didn't get to do often since they were usually too busy. In the past, they'd tell stories about their one-night stands or rib each other about their shitty choices in women. Today was different.

Asher refused to discuss his situation with Nikki, not until he figured his shit out for himself. Harrison insisted nothing had changed in his attitude about short flings, and there was no one special in his life. But his attitude was unusually curt, making Asher wonder what was really going on with Winter, the reporter. Zach, as always, claimed he got laid often enough and changed the subject to the bar. Which meant they talked about work.

★ ★ ★

TO ASHER'S SURPRISE, his father and Serenity returned early and joined them in the family room, where they laughed and reminisced about vacations they'd taken and stories about the triplets and the trouble they used to get into. And they promised to get everyone back here together sometime soon.

Asher caught sight of Nikki slipping past everyone and heading upstairs. Assuming she still needed time to process and wanted to avoid the family, he didn't call her back. Maggie was planning a special meal for Michael and Serenity's anniversary, and he knew she wouldn't miss it, if only to be polite. For now, she deserved some quiet alone time.

"Asher, can we talk?" his father asked, breaking into his thoughts.

Asher had been waiting for this conversation and rose to his feet. "Study?"

"Sure." Michael followed him as he walked out of the main area and toward the smaller room where they'd spoken with Derek this morning.

The dark wood floor-to-ceiling shelves held a variety of books for everyone's taste, from classics to mystery to romance and nonfiction. The chairs and sofa were a neutral-colored leather, and Asher sat beside his father on the soft-cushioned couch.

"I'm sorry." Knowing he was responsible for the need to talk, Asher spoke first. "I didn't even know the words were coming until I blurted them out."

Michael rubbed the back of his neck and sighed. "We should have discussed your mother and her illness," he muttered. "I wish I'd realized that years ago."

"You did the best you could."

Michael nodded. "I thought so at the time. But while living through Audrey's emotional crises, things were complicated. We were young. I was twenty-two when you were born, and I wasn't equipped to handle your mom's issues."

"Dad, you don't have to do this." Asher wasn't comfortable reliving those parts of his childhood any more than his father was.

"Yes, I do." Michael met his gaze and Asher saw the same-colored eyes as his reflected back at him. "Jade's issues made me realize I should have gotten help for you kids. I should have known she wasn't the only one impacted by your mother and my choices."

Jade suffered from migraines and anxiety, and when she realized she was pregnant last month, she'd panicked and come down to the island to be alone. Her baby daddy and now husband, Knox, Asher and Derek's close friend, had followed her and brought her home where they'd ended up in a family conversation that revealed old pain and hurt.

And here they were again, Asher thought.

"Audrey idealized being pregnant," Michael said. His expression grew distant, as if he was putting himself back in time. "She liked the attention she received, but when it came to being a mother and the responsibilities that came with it, she couldn't cope."

He paused and Asher remained silent, letting his father put his thoughts together.

"She wanted more kids and so did I," Michael said at last. "But I knew she couldn't handle the responsibility. You don't need to know the details, but suffice it to say, we had our children and loved you all. Your mother was just mentally unstable. No matter what I did to make things better, nothing worked."

Asher swallowed hard. Serenity had arrived when Asher was three years old. Even when his mother was still home, he remembered the dirty dishes stacked in the sink and the babies crying. No matter how often Serenity had cleaned, his mom added to her work. Yet Serenity had managed to care for all the kids and wrangle them as they got older. She handled children with ease and Asher had always felt torn, guilty for liking the nanny more than his own mother.

"I was nine when Mom walked out one day and never came back," Asher said. He'd wondered what he'd done wrong, and to make up for whatever it was, he'd stepped up to help with his siblings. So his father wouldn't leave next.

"By the time your mother left, Serenity had been with us for years." His father sat, hands clasped between his legs as he looked up at Asher. "I give you my word, I never looked at her as anything but the nanny when your mom was still home, or even right after she ran off. Our relationship started over a year after your mom's passing."

"I know that. I know the kind of man you are." Asher blew out a long breath. "But kids suck. I was twelve when you and Serenity married. People started talking the year before and it was tough."

"You never told me."

"I didn't want you or anyone else feeling bad." Asher shrugged. "Truthfully, I thought I'd put it all behind me. I love Serenity. Do I still struggle with some guilt because I think she was a better parent than Mom? Because I liked her better? Yes. But I'm an adult. I can handle it."

"Then what happened the other day? Was it just the comment about the age difference between you and Nikki that triggered you?" The small lines around his father's eyes seemed deeper, along with his concern.

"Nikki and I had talked about personal things. I guess it stirred up shit I never dealt with. Like I said, the words just came out. I didn't mean them. I can apologize again–"

Michael put a hand on Asher's shoulder. "Serenity let it go already. I would have except I'm worried about you. You're right about one thing. It was a hypocritical thing for me to say. I know from experience it's not an easy place to be, but if you love the girl–"

"Whoa, Dad." Love Nikki? Asher shook his head. It was way too fast to think such a thing. "You're getting way ahead of yourself."

"Am I? I've seen how you look at her."

Asher held up a hand but his father shook his head. "I need to finish. You have always put everyone's feelings before your own. Don't think I don't realize how you parent your siblings. It's second nature to you. And I am certain that's the hesitancy I see now. You're worried about what everyone else will think, and I didn't help that when I opened my big mouth." A wry smile lifted his lips.

Asher couldn't help but laugh. "No, you didn't." But his own smile quickly faded. "Add in Nikki is Derek's younger sister, and he already told me that he trusted me to take care of her? Nothing about Nikki and me is okay."

His dad steepled his forefingers and put them to his mouth, obviously giving Asher's words some thought. He lowered them to speak. "Maybe you should look at the situation with Derek another way."

Asher raised his eyebrows. "Yeah? How's that?"

"If Derek trusts you, it's because he thinks you're a good man. Even if your relationship with Nikki comes as a shock to him, given time, he'll come to see if he can trust anyone with his sister, it's you."

"It's something to think about," Asher said, ready to change the subject.

His father nodded. Always astute, he rose to his feet. "Let's go join the family, okay?"

Asher stood and his dad slapped him on the back.

"You can talk to me about anything. If you have feelings for Nikki, then give our talk some thought," Michael said and turned to walk out of the room.

Asher waited, taking a few minutes to gather his thoughts. Did he have feelings for Nikki? Without a doubt. Was he in love with her? The thought was enough to send him back to his family to avoid thinking about it. He was smart enough to know what the twisting in his stomach meant. He just wasn't ready to deal with it yet.

When he walked back to the family room, his father told him everyone had gone to their rooms to rest and get ready for the anniversary celebration later. His dad went upstairs to join Serenity, and Asher decided to head to his bedroom, too.

The tapping of dog paws caught his attention and he turned. Lucky walked over and nudged Asher's leg. "Why aren't you upstairs with your mother?"

"He was in the kitchen, begging for scraps as I cooked," Maggie said, striding past him. "I need to talk to Corey, but I'll be back in five minutes. Want me to take the dog with me?" she offered.

Asher shrugged. "Maybe he needs to go out. Thanks, Maggie."

"Come on, let's go," Maggie said, patting her leg to call the dog.

Asher stepped in the direction that led to his room, and Lucky trailed along beside him.

Maggie laughed. "Looks like you have a pal. If he wants to leave the bedroom, just open the door. He'll come find me in the kitchen."

She turned and strode toward the front door, leaving Asher to take Lucky with him. Once in his room, Asher pointed to the dog bed. "Go on. Settle in."

Jesus. He was talking to the dog like they were old friends.

The pup gave another whine and leaped onto the bed instead, curling up on the side where Nikki had slept. "Guess we know who's boss," Asher muttered. And for the first time ever, it wasn't him.

He was being led around by a woman he'd never expected and a dog he hadn't known he wanted.

His father's words came back to him again. What were his feelings for Nikki? Asher sat on the edge of the mattress and ran a hand over his face. The way the question kept popping into his head, he knew he had to face the answer.

He'd agreed to bring a beautiful young woman he believed to be a spoiled princess to his island home to escape trouble in the press she'd probably caused. Within an hour on the plane, he'd discovered she was intelligent and too damned chatty. He'd told himself she was driving him crazy, when in reality, he'd been both intrigued and amused by her personality.

He'd tried to paint her with the same brush as his shallow, cheating ex-model girlfriend and had been schooled by an honest apology and her zest for life. Though he had qualms about the age difference, they had more in common than not.

She couldn't trust people, making her a loner by nature. Though he had his tight-knit group of friends and family, Asher had the same issues trusting outsiders. They had both been dealt a raw deal with their parents, yet Nikki was an optimist. He, on the other hand, was more of a pessimist.

But she'd proven she liked him for himself, both his moody side and the lighter one he rarely showed, the one she easily coaxed out of him. In their few days on the island, she'd made him laugh and smile more than he'd done in the last year. She'd opened him up to see the world in a more upbeat way. When was the last time he'd played in the water? Meandered through town? Put up with a shedding dog in his bed?

He'd tried to resist her, but she'd charmed him and

left him wanting more and he didn't just mean in bed. He was attracted to so much more than her body, but he'd never connected with a woman during sex the way he had with Nikki. Their compatibility was off the charts. He'd looked into her eyes while buried deep in her body, and if he believed in soul mates, he'd swear he'd found his.

And if he ever discovered the person who'd violated her home, taken and sold the nude photos, and put the look of fear and humiliation in her expression? It would take all of his brothers and his best friends to hold Asher back.

He glanced at the dog, who stared at him through soulful eyes, and groaned. From the look of things, he was in love with his best friend's younger sister. What the fuck was he going to do about it?

★ ★ ★

TO NIKKI'S SURPRISE, she was able to put her problems aside and go downstairs for Michael and Serenity's small anniversary party. When she arrived, Harrison, Zach, and Michael were sharing drinks and laughing, lightening Nikki's heart. From the look of things, Asher and his father had patched up whatever issues and discomfort remained from yesterday's outburst.

She didn't want to bother them, nor did she see Serenity, so she walked toward the kitchen. The sound of female voices beckoned, and she stepped into the large room where Maggie stood, plating appetizers on a serving dish.

"Mmm. Smells good," Nikki said as she stepped into the kitchen.

Serenity turned. "Nikki, come join us." She tucked a strand of her black hair behind her ear and waved Nikki over.

"I wanted to see if I could help with anything," she said, joining them.

Serenity smiled. "I was asking the same thing, but Maggie insists on doing everything herself."

"Because it's your anniversary and Nikki is a guest." Maggie picked up the platter. "I'm going to see if the men are hungry."

"When are they not hungry?" Serenity asked with a smile.

Maggie chuckled and walked out.

"So, I heard you had a tough phone call this morning," Serenity said, pouring a glass of wine and passing it over to Nikki. "I won't pressure you but if you need a woman's shoulder, I'm here."

At that unexpected statement, Nikki picked up a glass and took a long sip. She met Serenity's warm gaze. "That's very kind of you, but I'm sure you don't want to hear about the mess I'm in." Nikki's own parents certainly didn't.

She hadn't heard from her mother since Derek had told her if she wasn't going to help then she should back off.

"What's wrong?" Serenity sat down on a leather-covered barstool and patted the seat next to her. "You look surprised."

"I guess I am." Nikki plopped herself onto the stool. "It's just that my family is very different from yours."

Serenity tipped her head to the side. "How so? I've seen your father on the news and caught sight of your mom from across the room at a luncheon, but I can't say I've met them in person."

"Then you're lucky." Nikki rested her arm on the cold granite countertop. Before Serenity could question her further, Nikki decided to blurt out the truth. "My parents, or at least my mother blames me for any situation I get myself into and this one? It may not be my fault, but the only thing my mother cares about is how it affects my father's campaign. Not me."

"But–"

Nikki shook her head. "No buts. She's upset with me," she admitted, pressing her palms to her red cheeks, embarrassed her own mother didn't care enough to worry about her.

"I'm sorry that's your experience, honey. But you've been around us long enough to know that's not who *we* are. We genuinely care about you. I know Zach is on the case. And Asher's there for you. I can see how he feels. It's in the way he looks at you." Her smile showed her approval of them as a couple. Another surprise.

Nikki swallowed hard. "I'm so grateful to all of you. But as for Asher, he's doing my brother a favor by having me here. I know we've grown close, but once we get back to reality, he's going to realize the pressure he's under. From my age to worry about letting my brother down…"

She shrugged, trying to make it seem like she wouldn't be devasted when the inevitable happened and he ended things. She was doing her best to think of Asher as her emotional support friend with benefits. Otherwise, the crash when it ended was going to be even harder.

Serenity shook her head, her disagreement obvious by the frown on her face. "Asher is stronger than you give him credit for. When he wants something, he goes after it." She placed her hand over Nikki's. "I want you to listen to me. Where you start out and where you end up are not always the same." She lifted her shoulder in a delicate shrug. "Look at me and Michael."

A lump rose to Nikki's throat. "I don't know that you can compare us that way, but thank you so much for your kindness. I don't mean to sound… well… pathetic, but I'm not used to that." Serenity was everything Nikki had always wished for in a mom, and she'd treasure these few minutes for a lifetime.

"Well, you should get used to it. No matter what happens in the future, you can come to us. To me. Do you hear?" Serenity tightened her hold to emphasize her point.

"Thank you."

Serenity smiled and released Nikki's hand. "Since I've taken you under my wing, I'm now inviting you to Nick and Aurora's baby shower so you can meet the rest of the family. Don't worry. Asher will be there, too."

"Asher's going to a baby shower?" Nikki asked, as the man in question joined them. In her nonexistent personal experience, baby showers were usually for women. At least, that's what she'd read in books.

Asher shrugged as he joined them. "Nick decided that he missed everything about Aurora's pregnancy the first time around. He doesn't want to miss a thing now, so it's a co-ed party."

Nikki smiled. "I love that for him. But I'm not sure I belong–"

"She'll be there," Asher said, wrapping an arm

around her shoulder. "Once Serenity adopts you, you're in for life."

Serenity, warmth emanating from her smile, nodded. "He's right."

"Okay. And thank you." Nikki couldn't remember the last time she'd felt so included.

"Good." She clapped her hands. "Now that that's settled, I'm going to find my husband and start celebrating our anniversary." She strode out of the room, leaving them alone.

Asher walked over to where Nikki still sat. "Are you okay?" he asked.

She nodded, overwhelmed but happy. "You're lucky," she murmured. "Your stepmother is a very special woman." She slid off the stool and Asher grasped her around the waist.

"*You* are a very special woman." He touched his forehead to hers. "Think you can put everything out of your mind and enjoy tonight?"

"Of course." For Asher and his family, she'd do her best. "Let's go celebrate."

She put her hand in his and they walked out of the room.

Chapter Eleven

THE NEXT MORNING, Asher woke up with Nikki in his arms. From what Zach had told him last night, Asher had a feeling today would be their last day on the island. His family was going home as planned, and after talking to Derek, Zach had suggested Asher and Nikki join them. Asher's intrepid brother had a plan and wanted to discuss it this morning. Since Asher was still in the dark, he hadn't mentioned anything to Nikki. They'd find out what was going on together.

After he'd found her in the kitchen last night, they'd enjoyed their evening, and he hadn't wanted to bring up anything that would remind her of her problems. Once his family retreated to their rooms, he'd lifted Nikki into his arms and carried her across the house and to his bed, where he'd proceeded to accept the words his father had put into his head.

He'd made love to her.

Although he'd kept the words to himself, he showed her in other ways. He slid into her slowly, built up her orgasmic tension, looked into her eyes, and any uncertainties about his feelings disappeared. She filled parts of him he hadn't known were missing. But according to Zach, their time together was coming to an end.

She might not be aware of what was coming but he was. Headed back home to her brother, her family, and the real world where Asher would have to make decisions. How did he intend to handle it?

He pulled her closer, breathing in the island scent of her hair, knowing he couldn't let her go, but keeping her wasn't a straight road, either.

The sound of banging startled him, and he jumped, causing Nikki to jolt. "What's wrong?"

"Wake up, you two. Meeting time," Zach called from outside the bedroom doors.

"Go get some coffee. We'll be there in half an hour," Asher called out.

"What time is it?" Nikki asked.

Asher glanced over her shoulder to the clock on the nightstand. "Eight o'clock."

She yawned, putting a hand over her mouth. "What does he want?"

Asher groaned. "Last night he told me he spoke to Derek. He thought we should fly home with the family. He wouldn't say why, so I figured we'd all talk about it this morning."

She nodded, her gaze steady on his. "What does this mean for us?"

"Time's ticking!" Zach yelled, and his footsteps sounded as he walked away.

Asher wanted to answer her but didn't know how. Not yet. "Let's see what Zach has to say? We can talk about everything after we know his plan."

Hurt crossed her features, the sparkle in her eyes shutting down. "Sure. Makes sense. I'm going to take a quick shower."

Before he could grab her, she rolled to the side of the bed, sat up, and climbed out. She walked to the chair in the corner and retrieved her clothes.

After waking up here the first morning after his family arrived, she'd stashed some items here that she could wear to go upstairs and not experience that walk of shame feeling. Her words, not his. Because she'd withdrawn into herself, he let her go.

Until he had an idea of what Zach knew, he couldn't make any plans or promises.

★ ★ ★

NIKKI SHOWERED AND dressed, then grabbed a cup of coffee in the kitchen, choosing the largest mug she could find to prepare for Zach's news. She was hurt that Asher hadn't reassured her about their relationship status once they returned home and now, she had to deal with everything she'd left behind.

She walked into the study, where Zach and Asher were waiting and decided to take control. "Okay, talk to me. What plan do you have so I can approve it or not?" Because at the end of the day, this was still her life, and she was going to make her own decisions.

"Take a seat and let's discuss." Zach gestured toward the couch next to where Asher sat.

Needing space to be able to think, she chose a large club chair and settled in.

Asher narrowed his gaze but said nothing.

"I have good news. I take it you haven't been keeping up with social media." He didn't phrase it as a question.

She shook her head. "Staying away. Far away."

"Then you should know there's a bigger scandal than you, and you've been knocked off the major headlines of most sites."

Nikki stared at him. "You're serious?"

"Deadly. A beloved, big-name actor cheated on his pregnant wife, and he now has two baby-mamas and babies on the way with both of them. In other words, the paparazzi have moved on. Derek said your building was quiet last night, and the doorman confirmed the same this morning. You can go home," Zach said.

Nikki knew she ought to feel relieved, but the anxiety rushing through her said otherwise. "But we don't know who set me up, so I can't just go on with my life." She nibbled on her lower lip, ignoring the fact that Asher's eyes remained glued to her face.

"Smart girl. The danger isn't gone but we need to draw this person out. So we are bringing you home… with a boyfriend."

Her stomach flipped at the word. "Boyfriend?"

A grin spread across Zach's face. "You and Asher are going home together to play boyfriend and girlfriend. Derek is packing up some things and dropping them off at Asher's place today."

Nikki shook her head, certain she was hearing wrong.

"What the hell? Derek knows? About the plan?" Asher's voice rose, and she couldn't tell if it was anger or panic.

Zach laughed. Nothing seemed to bother the man. "Relax. He thinks you two are coming home to engage in a fake relationship. Which, let's face it, won't be difficult for you two lovebirds to pull off."

Ignoring the fun he was having at Asher's expense, Nikki glanced at him. "So the purpose is…?"

"To give you a safe place to stay, to let whoever set you up know you're protected, and if they're keeping an eye on you, they'll know you are home and your apartment is empty. And I had Derek have a camera set up that'll tell us if someone tries to return for their equipment. Which reminds me. Call that friend of yours and let her know you're coming home and moving in with your new boyfriend."

"Giving her time to hang herself if she decides to come to the apartment for the camera," Asher said.

Zach nodded.

Nikki pursed her lips in thought. "Do I get a say in these plans?"

"Of course," Asher answered before Zach could.

As frustrated as she was with him for not answering her earlier question, she also had considered what Serenity said. About where things started and where they ended up. Living with Asher gave Nikki an opportunity to show him things between them could work in their real lives. It might be the only chance they had.

Eyes on her, Asher and Zach waited for her to speak. Zach was relaxed as always while Asher's shoulders were tense, his jaw rigid. In fact, he looked like he was about to launch out of his seat when she gave them a hard time. She had no doubt he thought she was annoyed with his reaction earlier.

Time to put him out of his misery. "I think it's a great idea," she said.

"You do?" Asher asked, shock evidenced in his wide eyes and stunned expression.

"I do. What time are we leaving?" She shot him a smile and rose from her seat.

"We'll leave for the airport around one," Zach said.

She nodded. "Then I'll go pack." She walked out of the room without explaining to Asher her reasons for agreeing.

Let him stew over whether she was upset with him or not and what to expect when they were alone in New York.

★ ★ ★

ASHER WATCHED THE wiggle of Nikki's ass as she left the room. Knowing it was the last thing he should be focusing on, he shook his head and groaned.

Meanwhile, Zach let out a laugh. "Took you by surprise, didn't she?" he asked.

"Yeah. I figured she'd argue about the arrangement." Zach had filled him in about the new scandal before Nikki joined them.

But the bastard had skipped the news that Derek already knew about the Asher and Nikki moving-in scheme, dropping the information like a bomb in the room. While Asher had been trying to figure out how to deal with Derek, Zach had known all along that Derek had agreed. Brothers, he thought and shook his head.

"Well, at least we don't have to deal with her making things difficult. So what's going on? It seemed like there was a lot of tension when she walked into the room. And she couldn't have chosen a seat farther away from you. What'd you do wrong?"

Asher rolled his eyes. "You are such a pain in the ass. I didn't do anything."

"Except?" His brother walked over and nudged Asher in the arm. "Come on, you can tell me."

"She asked what going home would mean for us. And instead of giving her a straightforward answer, I deflected."

"Oh, man."

Asher raised an eyebrow. "Like *you* know how to handle women?"

"Good thing we aren't talking about me." He grinned. "Here's the deal. We can all see how you feel about this girl. It's also obvious the age thing is as big an issue for you as Derek. Want my advice?"

"Why should I answer?" Asher rose from his seat. "You're going to give it to me anyway." And the truth was, he could use the advice even if Zach wasn't a relationship kind of guy.

"Derek will get used to it, and the age difference worked out well for Dad and Serenity. Not so much for you as a kid, but you're an adult now, so get your shit together. Nikki needs you. It's not like we're going home to a settled situation."

Unable to argue either point, Asher nodded before walking to his bedroom to get his things together for the trip home.

★ ★ ★

THE PLANE RIDE home was easy and everyone's mood was light. Asher's family talked, the brothers tossed insults, and nobody brought up Nikki's problems, for which she was grateful. Lucky had behaved, acting as if he were born to travel in style. He sprawled out on the floor in front of her seat and slept most of the trip.

She'd told Derek not to pick her up at the airport. Instead, she and Asher had made plans to meet him for dinner during the week. Since Zach had decreed she couldn't go home, she wanted to see if her brother had packed enough of her things for her to stay at Asher's. Otherwise, she'd be ordering online, because there were some items a girl couldn't do without. Her needs in the city were very different from those on the island.

Everyone had a driver waiting to take them home, so they parted ways in the parking lot. Serenity promised to keep in touch and insisted she'd see Nikki at Aurora's baby shower. Zach had hugged her and told her not to worry. He would come through and help her out. Though Harrison was preoccupied with something or someone on his phone, he'd also promised to talk to his partners about a job for her, had given her a brotherly hug, and told her to call if Asher fucked up. That had earned him a slap on the head from his oldest sibling, and Nikki laughed.

She, Lucky, and Asher loaded into the waiting vehicle. Asher was silent on the trip home, giving Nikki time to think. She felt odd being back in New York, and she missed the island already. The moment she'd stepped out of the plane there, she'd felt different. More at home. The warmth of the sun had called to her, and despite Asher's initial attitude, Maggie had welcomed her. He'd even lost some of his negative, grumpy personality. The longer they'd been together, the happier he'd become.

He spent the ride home talking to his assistant and other people from his office while she watched the scenery as it passed. Once at the building, he introduced her to Stan, the doorman, and put her on his permanent list of people allowed upstairs. He gave her a quick tour, and she loved the taupe, black, and cream masculine style of his living space. The furniture and decorative pieces were as beautiful as those on his island estate.

Despite being sure his cousin had been the decorator here, too, the place lacked a female touch. No photographs or knickknacks to warm up the space.

This was *Asher's* home whereas the Bahamas estate acted as the family retreat and had been decorated with lighter colors and many more personal pieces and pictures.

To her relief, Derek had dropped off her suitcases, and Stan had brought her things to the apartment. While Lucky sniffed his way around all the rooms, Asher picked up the heavier pieces of luggage and put them in his bedroom, giving her permission to move his things to make room for herself. In some ways, the gesture gave her hope, but she refused to focus on it until her personal problems were solved.

Asher left for the office to catch up on work, and the silence echoed around her. Knowing she had things to face here, too, she followed up with Meg by text. While on the island, at Zach's suggestion, Nikki had called to tell her *friend* she was coming home but wouldn't be staying at her apartment. Meg hadn't answered or called her back. Given Nikki's outburst during their last conversation, she wasn't surprised, so she texted Meg again with the same information and added an apology for the things she'd said.

Anything to bring an end to this situation. Nikki wasn't sure if Meg was capable of doing something as awful as photographing her nude and selling the images, but she needed to find out. Next, she shot off a text to Zach, informing him that she'd tried to reach

Meg twice. Even if the other woman didn't reply, at least they knew she was aware that Nikki's apartment was empty and thus fair game.

With nothing else to keep her busy, Nikki unpacked. She cleared one dresser drawer for her undergarments and hung up her clothes in Asher's large walk-in closet. In the bathroom, she spread out her toiletries on the counter and wondered how he would feel surrounded by all her bottles and makeup.

Lucky nudged her leg and she glanced down. "Hey. Do you want some water?" she asked the dog.

She stepped out of the bathroom and the pup followed her into the kitchen, where Asher had put the bag with Lucky's things. Nikki filled one of his bowls with water, placing it in an out-of-the-way spot, and he rushed over to drink.

She stored the dog food in the pantry, folded and placed Lucky's harness, leash, and other things on the counter, leaving a few toys on the floor against the wall for him to play with.

Asher hadn't complained about the dog coming back to his apartment, and she doubted he'd find Lucky or his things in the way. Lucky had become Asher's friend. One he'd let sleep on his bed, she thought with a grin. Nikki considered herself Lucky's person, Asher a close third because Maggie had been the dog's second favorite. The sweet woman might even have surpassed Nikki and kept the dog if she'd had the chance.

Nikki glanced at the pup as he drank his water. "I'll miss her, too," she told him.

As if sensing Nikki's need, he finished and walked over, rubbing his wet face on her bare leg. She knelt down to hug him, which he tolerated for a few seconds before he found one of his toys and walked out of the room. "Bye!" she called after him with a laugh.

Nikki took her phone off the counter and called Winter, wanting to catch up, but when the other woman didn't answer, Nikki left a message.

Which meant just one more person for her to reach out to. Gathering her courage, Nikki called her agent. With each message Amelia had left on Nikki's phone, her tone became edged with more frustration. Nikki shouldn't have avoided her for this long, but she hadn't been ready to make decisions about her life.

She was now.

Asher had once pointed out her age and how perhaps she didn't yet know what she wanted. There was truth in his words, at least when it came to her career. She had chosen modeling as a means of getting out from under her parents' roof, not because walking down a runway was her first choice. Just as pageants hadn't been something she'd loved, either.

Nikki had run to the island to escape the press and

pressure, but some good had come out of her trip. And she wasn't just referring to Asher. Her time there had allowed her to think about who she was and what she wanted out of life. The answer had become clear. Though she was still finding herself, she knew her current career path wasn't one she intended to pursue. Which put Harrison on her list of people to call this week.

She dialed and reached her agent's assistant, scheduling an appointment to meet Amelia during the week. Leaving her career wasn't something she could do over the phone. Nikki needed to face the woman in person, thank her, and inform her of her decision.

She looked around and felt like the walls were closing in on her. "Lucky, come!"

The dog came running, a stuffed animal in his mouth. "Let's go for a walk," she said, which had him dropping the toy and wagging his tail.

The sun shone brightly outside, and they walked for a while, taking a large square route that led her back to where she'd started. Her sweet boy had issues with his new environment. He'd peed on the sidewalk not the grass and trembled when they ended up in a tight group of people. She'd picked him up and carried him until they were alone again.

He'd adjust in time, she thought, kissing his head before putting him back down to walk. Before winter came, she'd have to get him sweaters because he was also used to the warmth of the island. She smiled at how cute he'd looked dressed up. Her boy would be a little stud.

At Asher's building, she smiled at the doorman as she passed him and led Lucky into the empty apartment, where she had to face the truth.

Despite being back in the city where she lived, Nikki felt very much alone.

★ ★ ★

THE FIRST WEEK back kept Nikki busy. Asher, too. Her sense of sadness over leaving the island faded as the week progressed. She didn't hear from Meg but at least Nikki's name had faded from social media.

Asher had been so tied up with business, he'd had to cancel their scheduled dinner with Derek, putting it off until next week. So she stopped by her brother's place for sushi, alone instead, bringing her dog with her. She'd ducked Derek's insistent questions about her time on the island with Asher and it hadn't been easy. Somehow, she'd managed not to reveal her feelings for her brother's best friend.

The meeting with Amelia had gone better than Nikki expected. Although she'd never gotten a maternal vibe from her agent, who was a ballbuster in business, Amelia showed up and hugged Nikki tight. She wasn't angry, as Nikki had thought she'd be, she'd been worried. And when Nikki told her she no longer wanted to model, Amelia understood. In personality, she'd reminded Nikki of Serenity and Nikki had once again seen the type of person her own mother should have been.

As for Asher, she'd settled into a routine, living with him, sleeping together at night, cooking him breakfast before he left for work. A routine she told herself not to get used to or count on. All she needed was a job, and Harrison said he'd introduce her to everyone at the baby shower and they could take things from there.

Despite telling herself much of her life now was temporary, and if she didn't think about the photos and who'd sent them, she was more fulfilled than she'd ever been.

★ ★ ★

ALTHOUGH NIKKI AND Winter attempted to make plans for lunch, they couldn't mesh their schedules until the morning of Aurora's baby shower. Since it was convenient, Nikki suggested they meet for an early breakfast at the hotel where the shower would take place, and Asher would meet her there in time for the event. The Meridian NYC was owned by Asher's family. Nick, Aurora's husband, managed the hotels around the country, and Nikki was looking forward to getting to know him and his wife.

Nikki chose a magenta dress with ruffled tiers from mid-thigh to the hem above the knee. The sleeves were a sheer balloon style with elastic around her forearm, and it had a sweetheart neckline. She adored the color, and when with her mother, she'd never been allowed to choose bright hues. Heaven forbid Nikki outshine Collette, who opted for pale pink, yellow, light blue, or ivory. Anything understated and, in her words, classy.

After finishing her makeup, Nikki walked out of the bathroom to find Asher lying on the bed, bare-chested and an arm propped over his head. One look at him and her heart beat faster.

He let out a low whistle of approval, telling her he liked how she looked, and she grinned. He crooked a finger, beckoning her to walk over. With her heels already on, she took delicate steps toward him.

"I got used to wearing flip-flops on the island," she said, making her way over.

His gaze turned hot, his eyes darkening. He grasped her hand and tugged, pulling her toward him. As soon as she was in kissing distance, she sealed her lips over his. He didn't wait, thrusting his tongue into her mouth and devouring her like he had last night. But at least then she hadn't been dressed and ready to go somewhere.

As he kissed her senseless, her nipples tightened, and she rubbed her thighs together in an attempt to alleviate the pressure suddenly building. But she needed to get going or she would be late.

"I have to go," she whispered against his mouth. She lifted her head and glanced at him. "Lipstick," she said, wiping the red color off the area around his mouth.

"Worth it," he said in a gruff voice.

"I'm guessing I need a touch-up, too." Her own voice was husky as well.

He nodded, his eyes dark with desire.

She retreated to the bathroom to fix her makeup, her body primed and she wished she could strip and climb back into bed with him.

Finally, she gathered her purse and left the apartment. She took a taxi to the hotel and arrived at the restaurant right on time, a miracle given the sexy distraction she'd had earlier.

"Nikki!" Winter called her name and she turned to see the other woman rushing toward her. "I hope I didn't keep you waiting?" Winter asked.

Nikki shook her head. "I just got here."

They hugged briefly as the hostess gathered two

menus and led them to a table by the window, placed down their menus, and left them alone.

"So how are you?" Winter asked. "You look tan," she said, smiling.

"I was on an island in the Bahamas."

"Oooh, nice. At least you were somewhere you could relax, though I'm sure it's been hard getting through the week."

Nikki nodded. "Both are true. The trip itself was amazing but overall it's been rough. But I've had good support from my brother and… friends." She used the term loosely because she'd had Asher, who was more than her friend, and she'd had his family there for her, too. There hadn't been anyone else.

Winter studied her for a long moment, her gaze narrowed and her expression astute. As if she were trying to read Nikki, her tone and body language.

"Any friend in particular?" she asked at last. "You said you were with your brother's friend, right?"

Nikki never had a woman she trusted to talk to about relationships. She was going to believe her gut and confide in Winter. "We're in a relationship," Nikki said. "I think. I mean we're together but it's private right now."

Winter leaned forward in her seat. "I'm listening."

"He has concerns about us."

"Like what?"

With a sigh, Nikki admitted, "My age and the fact that my brother is his best friend. Asher thinks I'm too young to be sure of what I want and that Derek will be furious after he trusted Asher to bring me to his island retreat."

Winter shook her head. "Men. They always think they know what's best for us. I don't care if you're twenty-one or thirty-one, you can make decisions for yourself."

"Agreed! And my brother doesn't get to dictate who I fall in love with…" She trailed off, realizing what she'd just admitted. "Umm, so yeah. That."

Winter's smile was warm and understanding. "I won't say a word. Just know I'm here to listen."

"Thank you. As soon as I find out who set me up and took the photos, I'll make my play. Right now I'm staying with him anyway. It gives me time to cement the relationship."

Winter laughed. "Something tells me the man won't know what hit him."

"That's the plan." Nikki could only do her best.

She and Asher had been sleeping together every night, unable to keep their hands off each other, and they spent time talking over breakfast and late at night. Either he felt the same way about her as she did about him, or he didn't.

"No matter what happens in the future, he's been

there for me in ways no one else has, and I will always be grateful," she said. Though the pain would be intense if he broke things off.

"Well, if he's a smart man, he won't let you go. I'm glad he's been there for you." She paused, then asked, "What about your parents?"

It was public knowledge who Nikki's mother and father were, so it wasn't a shock that Winter would ask. "They… aren't thrilled, obviously." She didn't know Winter well enough to go into a sob story about her relationship with them.

Winter picked up a water glass and took a sip. "I saw the press conference where your father refused to answer questions about the photos, and your mother requested they focus on political issues and not things that didn't impact them." Winter winced by way of apology.

Apparently, Derek had spared Nikki that information, and she swallowed over the lump in her throat. "My parents and I have a difficult relationship," she managed to say.

"Can I get you ladies drinks?" The server walked over, interrupting them.

Nikki glanced up. "I'll have a mimosa, please." If she was going to talk about her parents, some champagne would help. She looked at her friend. "Winter, want to indulge?"

"You know what? That sounds perfect."

The waiter tipped his head in acknowledgment. "Okay, I'll be back." He turned and walked away.

Before Winter could pick up the thread of conversation about Nikki and her family, Nikki decided a conversation change was in order. "What about you?" she asked. "How have your interviews with the owners of K-Talent been?"

"Very productive," she said. "Sasha and Cassidy are like sisters. They're so close and think alike. Their vision for the company is to showcase women, how they see the world, and how they are impacted by life. In my opinion, their movie choices are thoughtful as well as impactful."

Nikki smiled. "I love to hear that. I'm hoping to get a job with them. Oh! You didn't mention him but I know you interviewed Harrison Dare, too. I met him last week. I was staying at his brother's place, as a favor to *my* brother, and Harrison came down for his parents' anniversary. Anyway, he had very complimentary things to say about you."

Winter flushed and took another sip of her water. "We hit it off," she murmured, her evasive answer telling Nikki she was right in thinking something had happened between the two.

"Something you want to talk about?" Nikki asked, offering a shoulder in case Winter needed one.

The waiter returned. "Hello, again. Can I take your order?"

Winter shook her head. "We haven't had a chance to look at the menu yet. Can you give us some time?"

"Of course." He walked away.

Winter curled her hand around the water glass and met Nikki's gaze. "I slept with Harrison," she admitted.

Nikki blinked in surprise. Though she'd asked, she hadn't thought Winter would truly open up. "I thought he was a great guy. You two make a cute couple."

Winter shook her head. "That's not what it was. He made it clear he doesn't do relationships, and I was okay with that."

It was Nikki's turn to narrow her gaze. Winter said she *was* okay with that. Had something changed? Did she now want more from Harrison than he was willing to give? Or had Winter fallen for the charming actor/producer and he didn't reciprocate?

"So what changed?"

Winter shook her head.

Nikki opened her mouth but Winter jumped in first. "As much as I appreciate it, I'm not ready to talk about it yet. I need time to process my feelings, you know?"

"Makes total sense to me. I'm a processor, too. I

like to think things through when I can."

Winter nodded. "Are you ready to order?"

"Definitely or I'll be late for the baby shower."

For the next hour, they laughed and ate breakfast. Nikki kept her meal light so she'd be hungry at the party. After, she and Winter split the bill and walked out.

Once at the front of the hotel, she caught sight of Asher walking in, and she called out his name. He turned, saw her, and a bright smile lit his handsome features.

He headed toward her, and she was aware of other female eyes on him as he made his way over.

Winter leaned close. "He's got it bad for you," she whispered.

"Hi." Without glancing around, he leaned in and slid his lips over Nikki's, kissing her long, hard… and publicly for the first time.

By the time he stepped back, butterflies were in her stomach and desire rushed through her like it had this morning. She couldn't be near the man without wanting him.

"Introduce me to your friend?" Asher asked.

"I'm Winter Capwell." It was a good thing Winter had taken control of the conversation. Nikki was still too dazed from the kiss.

Asher extended his hand. "Asher Dare and I've

heard a lot of good things about you," he said.

They shook hands, and once introductions were over, Nikki had regained her composure.

Winter glanced at her phone screen. "I need to get going. It was a pleasure meeting you," she said to Asher.

"Same."

Winter walked out and Nikki met Asher's gaze. She was about to ask him what that public kiss had been about when a buzz of energy and people whispering sounded around them.

Nikki spun to see a crowd of well-dressed people walking their way and quickly realized her parents were leading the group. Big-money donors, no doubt, probably here for a luncheon.

"My parents," she said to Asher. Although her stomach cramped at the thought of dealing with them, they were in a public place. With so many people around, her mother wouldn't make a scene or call Nikki out for the scandal. She'd save that for the private dressing down.

"They're coming this way," Asher said.

"Which means we will have to say hello."

He slipped a hand into hers and she appreciated the support.

She took a step toward the approaching crowd, putting on her best pageant smile. "Mother," she called out.

Her voice could have gotten lost in the din, but her father must have heard her because he turned his head and met her gaze but her mother pulled on her husband's arm. Without a word, she steered the senator past Nikki, the large group following along with her.

Chapter Twelve

ASHER DIDN'T KNOW whose shock was greater. His or Nikki's. Her parents had dismissed her as if she were nobody. Beside him, she trembled, and he slid an arm around her waist before her legs gave out.

He was barely able to control his temper but confronting the senator and his wife now wouldn't help Nikki. She'd made it through two weeks after being splashed naked on social media without breaking down once. At least not in his presence. But the people who were supposed to protect her, care for her, and make sure the world didn't steamroll and hurt her had caused her to crumble. They ought to be ashamed of themselves and he wanted them to know it.

He led Nikki to the nearest bench and waited until they were sitting side by side so they could talk without anyone overhearing.

She glanced up at him, her wide green eyes glassy with unshed tears. "Well, that was mortifying." Her cheeks flamed with embarrassment.

"Their loss, baby. That was horrible but it's on them." And if he got ahold of them, he'd be only too happy to tell them all the wonderful things about their daughter they were too self-absorbed to notice. "Are you okay?"

She shook her head. "Not really. How could anyone be okay when their parents avoid them in public?"

Asher grasped her hands in his, but he had no words to make this better. All he could do was listen.

She looked down, as if unable to meet his gaze. "I always think I'm going to get used to them, but then they top what they did the time before." She swallowed hard, obviously holding on to her composure by a thread. "It's just… there's always that little girl in me who wants her mother's approval. I know she'll never give it to me, so why does it hurt so much each time she disappoints me?"

He slipped a finger beneath her chin and forced her to look up at him. "Because you're human? Because it's hurtful?" And because her mother was a horrible human being, but Asher didn't want to rub salt in an already open wound.

"You're right." Nikki glanced at her watch. "We should go. We're already a few minutes late for the shower."

He shook his head. "No. You don't need to put a smile on your face and fake being happy after what just happened. We're going home and I'll make an excuse for us later."

Nikki straightened her shoulders. "No. I'll stop in

the ladies' room and freshen up. Then we'll go celebrate Aurora's new baby."

If she was determined to attend, there wasn't much he could do.

She rose to her feet and he stood up beside her. "Do you have the gifts?" she asked.

She'd gone shopping during the week and purchased presents, helping him out, too. Otherwise he'd have asked his personal assistant to go shopping because he had no idea what to buy for a baby shower.

"The valet is having them delivered to the party," he said.

He walked with her to the restrooms and waited until she came back out. Her eyes were still red, but she was determined to put on a brave face and meet his family.

Her bravery was just one of the reasons he loved her. She thought of others even during her own trauma.

Once inside the party, Asher was determined to make pushing herself to attend worth her while. First, he walked her over to Aurora, Nick, and their daughter, Leah, and made introductions.

Asher's brother and wife were warm and welcoming as Nikki congratulated them. Then she looked at Asher's niece, who'd just given him a big hug.

"Hi, there. Are you excited to be a big sister?"

Nikki asked.

Leah wrinkled her nose. "It's getting a lot of attention and it's not even here yet."

Asher chuckled at her use of the word *it*. All the pink and blue balloons told them all they didn't know the sex of the baby.

"Leah's still unsure," Aurora said, putting her hand on her daughter's head. "She's been an only child for six years."

Nikki knelt down so she was eye level with the little girl. "Can I tell you a secret?"

Leah nodded, wide-eyed. "I'm the younger sister and you know what? I always wanted to be the big sister because my brother bossed me around."

Asher knew she was lying. She idolized her older brother, but she was doing her best to make things better for Leah. His heart, which already belonged to Nikki, swelled with pride.

"But, Leah, you get to be the oldest," Nikki said. "You'll be able to help your mom, be in charge sometimes, and either you'll have a sister who'll be your best friend one day or a brother who you'll love more than anything. Either way it's going to be great for you."

Leah was always a spitfire but she'd been more subdued today. She looked at Nikki warily, her eyes narrowed and distrusting. "Are you *sure*?"

Nikki nodded. "I have one more secret for you, okay?" She leaned in closer. "Sometimes, when you have a baby brother or sister, you get presents, too. In fact, your uncle Asher and I both bought you gifts."

Leah's eyes opened wide. "Really?" she asked, perking up and smiling.

"Really." Nikki rose to her feet. "But babies aren't just about getting presents. Remember, best friends one day." She winked at Leah, who was now bouncing up and down and ran to her grandparents, probably to tell them all Nikki's *secrets*.

"I don't know how to thank you for that. She's been in a grumpy mood all day," Aurora said, grinning.

Nikki shrugged. "She's adorable. I'm sure she's in a panic about losing her status as the favorite. She'll be fine when the baby comes."

"You're pretty amazing," Nick told her. He glanced at Asher and winked, giving Asher his younger sibling his seal of approval.

Asher's entire family knew he had something going on with Nikki. If he didn't tell Derek soon, he'd get his ass kicked twice and he'd deserve it.

He slid his hand into Nikki's and squeezed. "I want to take Nikki to meet Sasha and Cassidy, and you two have other guests waiting to say hello and congratulations." He tipped his head toward the people behind them.

He led Nikki toward Harrison's partners, determined to make sure she left here with a job. She deserved to have something positive come of this difficult day.

★ ★ ★

WHEN NIKKI AND Asher returned to his apartment, Lucky bounded to greet them. She knelt and buried her face in his fur, needing the comfort only a pet could give. Asher offered to walk him, and she was only too happy to take him up on it.

Later that night, Nikki and Asher made love. Despite the fact that the words hadn't been spoken between them, she refused to think of the act as anything else. She found solace with him in ways she'd never experienced before, and she held on while she could. Eventually, she slept, something that had become a regular occurrence with Asher by her side.

When she opened her eyes, Lucky was on the bed, which told her Asher had let the dog into the bedroom at some point during the night. He'd become quite the softy where the pup was concerned.

She'd woken up before him, which surprised her since she'd had a difficult time falling asleep. Her mind kept replaying the events of the morning with her parents, then the afternoon with Asher's relatives, who couldn't be more different than her screwed up family.

"What are you thinking about?" he asked from behind her, his voice gruff.

"I didn't know you were up."

"I could hear the wheels turning in your head," he teased.

Letting out a sigh, she admitted the truth. "I was just thinking about how my parents acted toward me and how much warmer your family is than mine."

He pulled her tighter against him, but his silence just meant he agreed and probably didn't want to speak and make things worse. She appreciated it. Her emotions were raw and hurt hovered at the surface. Tears threatened but she did her best not to let them fall, telling herself her mother and father weren't worth it.

"When I have kids, they're going to know they're loved," she said, her voice as fierce as she felt about the subject.

Asher stiffened behind her. Not wanting to freak him out or force a conversation he wasn't ready for, she dove into something else that had kept her awake last night. "I need to have a conversation with my mother."

"About what?" He pushed himself back up against the pillows and headboard, and she did the same.

"I quit modeling and I want to tell her to her face

that her choices aren't mine. I'm going to do what I want with my life."

Confusion etched his features. "After yesterday, why bother?"

She understood his reaction but he didn't know Colette Bettencourt. "My mother wants things her way. As in, she wants to be in control. Right now, she thinks I've been a bad girl and a disappointment, so she's punishing me. But once this scandal blows over—"

"Hasn't it already? That's why we came home," Asher said, obviously still struggling to keep up.

Nikki pulled up the covers a bit more, jostling the dog.

He jumped off and made his way to the bed Asher had put on the floor for him. One he rarely used.

"My mother can hold a grudge longer than the average news cycle keeps up with a story," she muttered. "But when she gives in and lets it go, she'll be happy to tell people her daughter is a model and name the high-end runways I've walked down."

Asher pinched the bridge of his nose and let out a disgusted groan. She patted his shoulder in understanding. "I know. Believe me, I know how ridiculous she is. Anyway, when I tell her I've fired my agent and quit? That she can't control me anymore? She's going to lose her mind." And Nikki couldn't stop the smile that took hold of her lips at the thought.

"You've got strength, growing up in that house," he muttered.

"I had Derek. Though she did try and control him during that period when he was engaged to that witch, thank God he came to his senses. But he's always been there for me."

Before Asher could reply, his cell phone rang. He leaned over and glanced at the phone on his nightstand. "It's Zach."

"Take it. Maybe he has news." She clutched the comforter in her hand.

"Hey. Tell me you have news for Nikki?" Asher said. He paused, obviously listening. "Sure. Hang on." He glanced at her. "I'm putting him on speaker so you can hear."

She nodded and grasped Asher's muscular forearm, holding on for dear life.

"Go ahead, Zach. We're both listening."

"Hey there, pretty girl. It was good to see you at the shower yesterday," Zach said.

Asher rolled his eyes. "Quit the flirting and just tell us what you found out."

Flattered, Nikki laughed. "It was good to see you, too, Zach."

"Okay, so I have big news. And I hate that I have to be the one to tell you, but it was your model friend and your ex, Lance Freeman."

"What? How is that possible?" she asked.

"Do they know each other?" Asher put an arm around her.

"They do. Through me. But they didn't like each other and made it a point to tell me that often." She pursed her lips and gave her own words some thought. "Which they would have done if they were working against me. But Lance and I have been apart for over six months. Wouldn't he have acted sooner?"

"Not if they were playing a long game," Zach said.

Asher met her gaze. "What do you mean?" he asked his brother.

"Okay, so you already said this Meg person was jealous of you, right? And if Lance was upset with you for some reason, they could have been working against you, setting you up. Don't forget, if those photos surfaced six months ago, Lance would be the prime suspect. Waiting makes sense. As in playing the long game."

Asher murmured in agreement with his brother.

Nikki, meanwhile, had chills from this whole conversation. "What did you find out?" she asked Zach. "How do you know it was them?"

"I put a PI friend on their trail. Turns out the studio where you had that fashion shoot and lost your keys? They had security cameras everywhere but the dressing rooms. And my friend was able to get ahold of the footage. He saw Meg digging through a bag that fit the description you gave me."

She and Zach had talked. Rather he'd questioned her about anything he thought could be a lead to whoever had set her up, and she'd answered as best she could.

"A different camera caught her meeting a man matching Lance's description by the front doors and handing him something. A couple of hours later? He returned that something to her. We didn't see her putting anything back in the bag because it had been moved. But it's pretty obvious she took your keys, he made a copy, and you can figure out the rest. The doorman confirms your boyfriend came and went *after* the date you said you two broke up. You hadn't removed his name yet."

"I forgot," she whispered. "I did it at least a month after I ended things." She put her face in her hands, and Asher ran his palm over her back.

"What matters is that we have them arrested for what they did," he said, doing his best to keep her calm.

Zach's groan traveled over the speaker. "And that leads to the not-so-good news. Depending on what they get charged with, we're talking up to one year in jail and if there's no criminal history? They may not even serve time."

She let out a sigh.

"One way or another, they will pay. Just not for as long as we'd like."

She lifted her head a blew out a long breath. "That's so unfair."

"But better than nothing," he said. "So here's the next question. How do you want to handle it? I can turn all the evidence over to the police. I'm sure they'll take your statement, but eventually you can wipe your hands of the two dirtbags, let it go, and live your life. That is the best revenge."

Asher nodded. "Their careers will be ruined and their reputations destroyed. That's something, at least. Nikki? Your call."

"Let the police deal with them," she muttered.

"Agreed. Okay, kids. I'm going to walk the evidence into the police station myself. I'll be in touch," Zach said.

"Zach, thank you. I appreciate everything you've done to help me."

"My pleasure, pretty girl. Bye, Ash." Zach disconnected the call.

Asher hit the end button on his phone. "The way he talks, you'd think he was the older brother. But he does get results." He turned to her. "Are you okay?"

She managed a nod. "It hurts but at least I know.

From Meg, it's not as much of a shock as it is from Lance." She might never know why he'd targeted her.

She tossed the covers off her lap and slid out of bed.

"Where are you going?" he asked.

"To shower and get ready to face my mother. I might as well do it when my adrenaline is pumping anyway."

She walked through his room, picking out her clothing, Lucky watching her from his place on the floor. Facing her mother required she be herself, and she pulled out items that represented who Nikki Bettencourt was and not who her mother preferred she be.

"Do you want backup?" he asked.

She swallowed hard. "That's sweet but this is something I have to do myself." Her mother needed to see she could stand on her own. "But I'm grateful for the offer."

He nodded. "Any time."

Or not.

She was well aware this was probably her last day or two staying with Asher. Once Meg and Lance were arrested, there was no reason for her to avoid her apartment. But leaving wasn't something she wanted to bring up. She had enough weight on her shoulders without a confrontation about *their* relationship.

One thing at a time, she thought, as she stepped into the bathroom and shut the door. First, her mother. Maybe someday, Meg and Lance. And too soon, she'd have to say goodbye to Asher.

★ ★ ★

NIKKI WALKED UP to her parents' door and rang the bell. She knew they were home because she'd called and spoken to the housekeeper, who answered the landline. She didn't want to give her mother a heads-up about her arrival. Though she was angry with her father, she viewed him more as a pathetic man who allowed his wife to lead him around and dictate his moves, but her mother? She was the puppet master and Nikki had had enough.

To her surprise, her mother opened the door, and if the open-mouthed expression on her face was any indication, the housekeeper hadn't given her a warning that her daughter was stopping by.

"Hello, Mother." Without waiting for an invitation that might not be coming, Nikki brushed past her and strode inside.

Her mother shut the door behind her. "Nicolette, what are you doing here?"

"Because I wasn't invited, you mean? Just like you couldn't be bothered to acknowledge me in public?"

Nikki caught sight of the family's new-to-her housekeeper hovering at the end of the long hallway and inclined her head in greeting. "Do you want to have this conversation in private or where *the help* can hear?" she whispered that last part to the woman who cared what other people thought.

"Let's take this in the study." Collette walked in the direction of that room, and Nikki followed into the room with dark wood furniture, heavy drapes on the windows, and an imported Persian rug on the floor.

"I hope you're not here expecting an apology, because surely you understand being seen with you isn't good for your father's potential campaign. We were with very important donors," her mother said, her gaze raking over Nikki for the first time. "What are you wearing? Who goes out of the house in that?"

Nikki glanced down at her black yoga pants, fitted tank top, and white Chucks. She had no makeup on and her hair was up in a messy bun. The way most women walked around these days.

Nikki looked at her mother, wearing a Chanel skirt and jacket and equally expensive shoes, and said, "I'm wearing what I want. Now let's go back to your first question about whether I'm expecting an apology. Not only do I not expect an *I'm sorry*, I don't expect or want anything from you. Or Dad."

Collette fingered the pearls around her neck, making Nikki wonder if her mother was nervous or just wanted this talk over with.

"Tell me something," Nikki said. "Why did you have children? Did you look ahead, knowing you wanted to be First Lady, and realize that you needed the two kids and proverbial white picket fence?"

"I—"

Nikki waved a hand in front of her. "You know what? Never mind. Don't answer that. I'm not even sure I care. I'm here to tell you I quit modeling."

"You did what?" her mother's voice rose in disbelief.

Nikki felt her heart beating wildly in her chest. Confrontation didn't come easily, but she couldn't be her own person if she didn't get through this moment and then face the two people she hoped would be arrested soon.

"I. Quit. Modeling." She repeated herself, feeling freer as she did. "I'd ask why you care what I do but I already have it figured out. You want what I do with my life to make *you* look good, and I'm done trying to please you when I've gotten nothing in return. Just know that you can't control me anymore. You can't brag about me when I perform to your liking and ignore me when I let you down, which, let's face it, is more often than not."

Her mother shook her head, disappointment oozing from her pores. "You never appreciated what your father and I gave you. The money we spent, the opportunities you had."

Nikki shook her head and drew a deep breath, ignoring the nausea that threatened. "I could argue with you all day but there's no point. Just know you didn't give me the true things I needed from you. Your love and approval, and I've learned those are things I will never get. Not from you."

Collette didn't even have the grace to look apologetic for the behavior Nikki called her out on. "This shouldn't come as a surprise to me. You always were needier than your brother," she said, raising her chin as if Nikki's words had no impact.

"Let's make things simple. From now on, I don't exist for you, which shouldn't affect you given how you treated me yesterday."

"You're going to regret throwing away a lucrative modeling career," her mother said, obvious disdain in her tone.

Nikki shook her head, feeling sad for this woman who put appearances and bragging rights above her own kids' happiness. "The only thing I regret is not putting my foot down with you sooner. The only reason I became a model was to gain my financial freedom. Not to give you something to brag about when it suited you. I can take care of myself."

Her mother let out a dry, almost mocking laugh. "Really, what else do you think you can do with your life?"

"I'm not sure, since it's always been dictated for me, but I'm ready to figure it all out, on my own and without your influence."

It felt good to say the words and she knew they were true. She had her whole life ahead of her, and she was excited to see what awaited her. "I came to have my say, I did, and now I'm leaving." She turned, stunned to see her father standing in the doorway.

"Nicolette," he said, sounding stunned. His eyes wide, he'd obviously overheard enough.

She met his gaze, hoping he'd defend her, but he remained silent. The same as always. Her mother's word was law. Nikki had expected it, but his inability to stand up to his wife on behalf of his daughter hurt anyway. If Nikki disappointed her mother, it was her father who'd let Nikki down by letting Collette dictate his relationship with his children.

She walked past him and out the door, proud of herself for finally taking control of her life. Even if she did climb into her car, start the engine, drive around the corner, and pull over to the curb for a good, long cry.

Nikki returned to Asher's apartment, aware of her red-rimmed eyes. She recounted the confrontation, pacing while she told Asher the story, and when she was finished, he applauded.

"I'm so damned proud of you," he said, rising from his seat on the sofa in his main living area.

She smiled. "I'm proud of me, too. I called Derek on my way home and told him everything. He said it was about damned time."

"How about we go out to dinner to celebrate?" Asher asked.

She shook her head. "To be honest, I'm exhausted and I'd rather just order in."

"Whatever you want," he said.

She nodded, grateful. What she wanted was a nap so she could decompress, food in a relaxed setting, and to crawl into bed with Asher.

One of his best qualities was that he never said what he didn't mean. Even on the plane when he'd told her she talked too much, he hadn't held back. If he minded staying home tonight, he'd say so.

But that was just it. This apartment wasn't her home, but Meg and Lance hadn't been arrested yet. She felt safer here, and if Asher wasn't going to ask her to leave, she wouldn't mention it yet. She still had time to be with him before she packed and moved back to her apartment. A place she associated with being violated, where she didn't want to live any longer.

Asher held out his hand and she took it, drawing strength from his presence. "Why don't you go take a shower and then lie down," he said, as if reading her mind.

She stepped closer and wrapped her arms around his waist, holding on tight. He always seemed to know what she needed and right now, she needed him.

Chapter Thirteen

A COUPLE OF days after Nikki told off her mother, Asher sat at Serenity's favorite dessert café, waiting for his stepmother to walk in. Nikki had been acting off and he wasn't sure what was bothering her. Maybe it was the fact that Meg and Lance hadn't been arrested yet, but the police were talking with the district attorney and cementing their case prior to arresting the duo. Asher was sure Zach had had a lot to do with how things would play out. His brother had contacts everywhere, and he'd make sure to take care of Nikki.

Asher glanced up as the hostess led Serenity to the table. He rose to greet her. Serenity, dressed in a pair of navy slacks and heels and a soft-looking cream silk sleeveless blouse, walked over and pulled him into a hug. "I was so happy you called," she said as she sat down, picked up the napkin, and placed it on her lap.

He did the same. "I'm glad you were free."

She smiled. "I've always said, nothing is more important than my kids."

That right there. Her huge heart was why his father loved her. Why most of his siblings that weren't biologically hers called her Mom.

And why he was here with her now. He had a couple of reasons he wanted to meet her and he'd be lying if he said he wasn't nervous. He'd put together huge acquisitions to make the Dirty Dare brand the competitor in the marketplace it was today, yet facing this delicate woman had his insides trembling.

"Can we talk?" he asked.

She nodded. "Of course. But do not apologize for what you said one more time, because it's over and done with."

He felt heat rise to his cheeks, as it did any time he thought of that outburst. "Okay, then let me just say I did you a disservice all these years. As the oldest, I was the one who remembered having Audrey around. And accepting you as my mother felt disloyal." He shook his head. "I was wrong. She was my mother in name and by blood and she suffered with mental illness, but even when she was around, you were the one who raised us. Made sure we got to school. Took us clothing shopping. You deserved better from me."

Asher didn't just realize it after what he'd said to her on the island but from how Nikki's parents treated her. He could have been nicer to Serenity over the years. Kinder. Warmer.

"Asher, please. You don't have to do this. But thank you for saying it anyway. And thanks for always looking out for the family. It hasn't gone unnoticed how you step up."

He let out a relieved breath, glad the hardest part of today was over.

"You said there were a couple of things you needed to talk to me about?" Serenity asked.

A waiter walked over and Asher shook his head. "A few more minutes, please." He paused until the man walked away and glanced at Serenity. "After we finish eating, would you be available to go ring shopping with me?"

She clapped her hands in glee, then looked around to make sure she hadn't caused a scene, laughed, and placed her hands in her lap. "Of course! I'm so honored you asked me."

Having Serenity join him made sense. As a woman, she'd have an idea of what he should buy, but more importantly, it was a step toward bridging the gap he'd caused between them.

"I figured you'd be a bigger help than Harrison or Zach," he said with a wry laugh.

She chuckled and took a sip of the water from the goblet on the table. "I'm so glad you got past whatever was holding you back."

He blew out a breath. "Well, the age thing, taking a step back and thinking about you and Dad over the years helped. Plus, I'm not going to push her to rush into anything. She needs time to figure out all the parts of her life."

Serenity nodded. "That makes sense."

"As for the other issue, her brother, Derek, is my close friend, and he sent me to the island with Nikki to look out for her. I'm pretty sure there will be fireworks before we come to terms. Or rather before *he* accepts us as a couple." Asher shrugged. "I'll take the punch if that's what I need to do."

Her eyes opened wide. "He wouldn't." She waved a hand in front of him. "Never mind. I don't want to know. Men," she muttered, picking up the menu. "Now, let's eat so we can get to the fun part and go jewelry shopping."

Asher leaned back in his chair and smiled. He was looking forward to it, as well. What was he dreading? The conversation he intended to have with Derek immediately after.

★ ★ ★

RING IN HIS pocket, Asher gave the doorman his name. He'd texted Derek and let him know he was stopping by and made sure his friend was home.

Asher took the elevator to the top floor to find Derek waiting with his door open.

"I was surprised you wanted to come over. What's

up?" Derek stepped aside for Asher to walk by and, once he did, shut the door behind them.

"I needed to talk to you, face-to-face."

Derek gestured to the living room. They walked into what Asher joked was the man-cave and sat down on the sofa. The television was on. Derek picked up the remote and hit the off button, placing the control back onto the table.

He turned toward Asher. "I need to thank you for pulling Zach in on Nikki's situation. He knew exactly how to get the information to figure out who was tormenting her and I'm grateful." He slapped Asher on the back. "I owe you one."

Asher was about to call in that marker and hopefully save himself a black eye. "I'm always here to help you, but I'd do anything for your sister."

Derek stilled. He narrowed his gaze, his sudden wariness obvious. "Okay, why are you here, and you'd better not tell me you fucked around with my sister."

Asher blew out a long breath and shook his head. "I wouldn't play games with her." He chose his words carefully.

"Not an answer." Derek opened and closed his hands into fists while his face turned an angry shade of red.

Asher wrapped a hand around the back of his neck and massaged the tense muscles, wondering how to defuse Derek's anger long enough to get him to listen. "How long have you known me?" he asked his friend.

"Long enough to know something's up I'm not going to like."

Asher had given this conversation plenty of thought. How to broach the subject, how to get his feelings across when he'd never been one to express his emotions to a friend. Faced with the moment, everything he'd considered saying flew out of his head.

He stood up, reached into his pocket, pulled out the ring box, and popped the top.

"What the hell is that?" Derek all but shouted. "Stupid question. You'd better start from the beginning and explain before I knock out your teeth and make talking impossible."

Because he wanted to keep his teeth intact, Asher decided to start at the end and work his way back. "I love her. Before I tell you anything else, you need to know that."

Derek paced.

Asher snapped the box closed and shoved it back into his pants pocket. "We both know Nikki is a beautiful woman."

"She's a twenty-one-year-old girl," Derek said through clenched teeth.

"She's an of-age, legal, beautiful woman. I noticed and tried to keep my distance—"

"Obviously not hard enough." Derek's eyes might as well be active lasers, the way he glared at him.

"Look, your sister is special. She has a way of inserting herself into people's lives and changing them for the better."

Asher recalled the deep conversations they'd had, how he'd opened up to her when he normally never talked about any parts of his past. He remembered the shopping trip in town and her excitement at the smallest of things. "I let her put a dirty, stray dog in my SUV, for God's sake. There's nothing she could ask for that I wouldn't do."

"So you slept with her." Derek's posture was brittle.

Asher closed his eyes and opened them again. "I don't think you or I want to have that conversation."

"Fuck!" Derek raised a hand, and Asher was afraid he'd slam his hand into a wall before he saw reason and lowered his arm. "You're a playboy, Asher. You find a woman, fuck a woman, and move on."

Asher groaned, unable to deny his friend's words had once described him. "That *was* me. I'd been used and hurt. I didn't want to open myself up to another woman ever again, but Nikki isn't just any woman. She got inside my head and helped me heal parts of my past I thought I'd carry forever. I'd like to think I helped her do the same."

"My mother," Derek muttered. He rubbed his palms against his eyes. "Something in your relationship gave her the strength to take a stand and confront her and to quit modeling."

"I'm sure your parents ignoring her in public was the trigger for ridding herself of your mother. The bravery was all Nikki. But if her knowing I had her back helped, then I'm glad. Nobody should be subjected to that bitch." Asher didn't apologize for what he'd called Derek's mother, and his friend didn't flinch.

"I always did my best to protect her," Derek said, more to himself than to Asher.

"And Nikki loves you for that. She idolizes you. If you don't give your approval about us, I don't know what she'll do. Forcing her to choose isn't fair. She needs you in her life."

And Asher needed Nikki in his. He hoped the reverse was true, too. For her sake, this discussion had to result in an understanding.

Derek turned toward him. "Asher, you've been my friend for years. I trusted you not to hurt her—"

"And I haven't."

Derek held up one hand. "I also trusted you not to go *there*." He winced and went on. "That said, I know you're a good guy, a decent man. My sister could do a lot worse except... she's *twenty-one* and has barely started her adult life."

"I know that." Asher walked over to his friend and placed a reassuring hand on his shoulder. "I bought the ring because I don't want to live without her, and I need her – and you – to know that. Personally, I'd marry her tomorrow. But that's not what I'm going to ask her to do."

Derek narrowed his gaze. "What do you mean?"

"I've already thought about her age, how many choices lie ahead for her, how much she could still do before settling down. If she says yes, the timing is up to her. Six months, five years, as long as she's got my ring on her finger and I know we're a team, she decides when we take the next step. I want her to have all the choices and life experiences that you do."

Much of Derek's anger had already begun to deflate, and at Asher's explanation, his shoulders dropped and his posture relaxed. Signs he'd begun to, if not accept Asher and Nikki, then resign himself to the idea. "You've obviously thought this through."

"I have. If it helps you to know, I fought myself, my loyalty to you, and my worry about our age difference the whole time. But Nikki, she's a force of nature. I can't not love her so please don't ask me to." Asher waited a beat for his words to sink in before hitting harder. "If you do force me to choose, I can't say you'd win. And I already told you I don't want to put her in the middle of the two most important people in her life."

Derek let out a wry laugh and Asher felt his tension ease. "Think that much of yourself, huh?"

Asher grinned. "I can't help it if she finds me irresistible."

"Gross."

"Seriously. You're the only person who gives her the respect she deserves. You're one of my closest friends, so I came to you man to man. I want to marry your sister and I'd like your blessing—rather than your fist in my face." Asher extended his hand.

Derek eyed him warily. "I grew up with her. I hope you know what you're getting yourself into," he said, extending his arm and shaking like they'd settled a deal. "I can't say I'm all in or I don't need time to adjust, so can you watch the PDA around me?"

Asher let out a laugh. "That I can do."

★ ★ ★

ASHER HAD GONE to spend the day with Serenity, talking and making amends, as he'd called it. No sooner had he left than Nikki's cell rang, Zach's name flashing on the screen. Lucky, who'd been lying on the floor in the kitchen, perked his head up at the sound.

Curious, she answered right away. "Hello?"

"Hey there, pretty girl. I have good news."

Knowing any news he had involved the photos, Meg, and Lance, Nikki's stomach did a flip. "What is it?"

"Your exes, friend and boyfriend, were arrested this morning."

"Oh, wow." She wasn't sure whether she felt more relieved or sad. Either way, the end result was for the best. "What happens now?"

"I wish I could say it was over for you but probably not. I'm sure they'll both hire lawyers, even if it's a public defender. If they take a deal, you're off the hook. If they want to go to trial, you might have to testify. The DA will be in touch."

"I understand." She'd do whatever she had to. "Can you tell me where they were taken? I need to see them." She had to know why they'd targeted her. What each of them had against her. Then she could put the whole nasty business behind her.

"Wish I could but not even my skills and contacts can get you around state law. Only an attorney can see a defendant. Once they make bail you can talk to them. Sorry, hon."

"Zach, who are you with your *skills and your contacts*?" she asked.

He let out a laugh. "Just your everyday bar owner."

Yeah, right, she thought, amused. "Thanks again,

Zach."

"Of course. Make sure my brother's taking good care of you. Talk soon." He disconnected and she shook her head. Whatever woman ended up with Zach would have her hands full, but she'd also be a lucky lady.

Nikki looked around the kitchen and sighed.

This was it.

Meg and Lance had been arrested, and whatever happened to them, she was safe and could go home. There was no reason to stay with Asher any longer. She shivered, deciding that she wasn't going back to the place where she'd had her privacy invaded and she no longer felt safe. She would just show up on her brother's doorstep and stay with Derek while she looked for a new apartment.

Nikki put the last of her clothes in the suitcase she'd placed on Asher's bed. Her shoes were on the bottom, and all she had left to add were her toiletries from the bathroom and Lucky's things. The first time she'd picked up a toy and placed it in the suitcase, he started to cry and carry on, so she dropped the bone back on the floor, leaving his things for last.

The dog lay on Asher's side of the bed, looking up at her with soulful eyes, as if he knew what she was doing and why. Maybe he sensed her mood, her lack of enthusiasm for leaving, and the dread she felt about saying goodbye. But she'd never walk out without thanking him for all he'd done.

From agreeing to take a woman he didn't know to his personal island retreat to indulging her whims, from playing in the ocean to trips to town, jet skiing and letting her bring a dog home, he'd been amazing.

"I mean, sure, we had a rocky start," she said, talking to said dog. "But we really got to know each other. And in the end, him believing in me helped *me* believe in and stand up for myself." Those were things that could never be repaid.

Asher had even let her stay in his apartment since they'd returned from New York. Their relationship had run its natural course. It wasn't his fault she'd fallen in love with him.

Lucky howled. She'd swear the dog was a mind and mood reader.

"It'll be okay," she told him. "We'll have each other and we'll get through the pain." Eventually.

She sighed and walked toward the bathroom with a small bag to put her toiletries into. She added her lotions and makeup pouch, her toothbrush, shampoo and conditioner, and whatever else she could find that belonged to her.

She glanced around the countertops and inside the shower. "Looks like that's it," she said to herself, the lump in her throat growing larger. She just needed to get through a little while longer without breaking down. She could cry all she wanted when she settled into Derek's guest room.

She shut off the light and stepped out of the bathroom to find Asher standing by the bed, staring at her open suitcase.

"What is that?" he asked.

She tipped her head to the side. "My suitcase," she said, as if it were obvious. Because it was.

"I got that. *Why*?"

"Didn't Zach call you? Meg and Lance were arrested."

He nodded. "I got the message on my way home. I'm still not seeing the correlation."

She'd never known him to be dense. "Asher, we agreed to be together on the island. In fact, I had to convince you to keep things going once your family arrived. I was staying here so whoever planted the camera and sold the photos knew I was protected and they couldn't get to me. That's all over now."

"So you're leaving? Just like that?" He snapped his fingers, the sound echoing around her.

"A couple of days ago, Zach told us who was behind the pictures. I knew then our time together was coming to an end. I thought you would say something. You didn't mention me leaving, but you didn't ask me to stay, either. I don't want to take advantage. You've done more for me than anyone I know and more than I can repay."

And the last thing she ever wanted was for him to resent her for overstaying her welcome.

★ ★ ★

ASHER DROVE HOME on a high. Engagement ring in his pocket, Derek's blessing – or as close to it as he could get for now – giving him a boost, he was mentally planning when and how to propose. He wanted Nikki to know he'd given the moment the seriousness it deserved. Until he walked into his bedroom to the sight of her suitcase, packed full of her clothing, open on the bed.

His insides twisted into knots. Lucky trotted up to him, nudging his leg with his nose. "Don't worry, boy. You're not going anywhere."

The time frame for his proposal had just been moved up. If he believed she wanted to leave, he'd swallow his pride, step back, and let her go. He knew better.

Just then, she strode out of the bathroom, wearing a pair of leggings and one of his oldest tee shirts, cementing his gut feeling. She was as attached to him as he was to her.

"What is that?" he asked, staring at the piece of

luggage on the bed.

She tipped her head to the side. "My suitcase." She stated the obvious.

And it wasn't what he'd meant. "I got that. *Why*?"

"Didn't Zach call you? Meg and Lance were arrested."

He nodded. "I got the message on my way home." He'd been too busy choosing the perfect diamond to answer his phone. He glanced at her. "I'm still not seeing the correlation," he said when in fact, he understood completely. He wanted her to spell it out for him so he could tell her just why she was wrong.

"Asher, we agreed to be together on the island. In fact, I had to convince you to keep things going once your family arrived."

Because back then he was still coming to terms with the notion that he'd found *the one* and not only was she too young, she was his close friend's sister.

She watched his face as she spoke. "I was staying here so whoever planted the camera and sold the photos knew I was protected and they couldn't get to me. That's all over now."

"So you're leaving? Just like that?" He snapped his fingers loudly.

"A couple of days ago, Zach told us who was behind the pictures. I knew then our time together was coming to an end." The light in her eyes dimmed and he wanted to pull her into his arms, but he waited. "I thought you would say something. You didn't mention me leaving, but you didn't ask me to stay, either." Her shoulders lifted in a small shrug. "I didn't want to take advantage. You've done more for me than anyone I know and more than I can repay."

He blinked, realizing how badly he'd handled things between them. Instead of setting things up ahead of time, he should have told her how he felt. He grasped her forearms and walked her to an empty place on the mattress and pushed her to a sitting position.

"We need to get something straight."

"What is it? What's wrong?" Concern lit up her pretty features.

He could go through all the ways he'd screwed up. He could explain he hadn't told her his feelings because he wanted to square things with her brother. But explanations could all wait.

He slid a hand into his pocket, pulled out the box, and dropped to one knee.

Her sweet mouth opened. "What are you doing?"

He flipped open the jewelry box. "Nikki Bettencourt, you barged into my life and showed me there are colors where I saw black and white. You taught me to have fun. Being around you healed the rift I created within my family. One I didn't even know was there.

You made me a better man and I don't want to live without you."

Not bad for off-the-cuff, he thought.

"Asher," she whispered, her eyes darting from the radiant-cut diamond, one he'd chosen because the jeweler said it was perfect for women who were bubbly and outgoing, and the stone was radiant, like Nikki.

"Before you answer me, I have a few more things to say."

Tears – he hoped they were happy tears – filled her eyes as she nodded.

"I know we've talked about our age difference and how at twenty-one it's hard to know what you want. Well, you're different, as you reminded me. And I believe you know your own mind. I trust that if you say yes, you're all in. But *you* need to know you have all the time in the world before you have to think about a wedding. You can experience the world, go to school, work in film, build a career, do anything you want. When you're ready to get married, I will be here."

She blinked and those tears trickled down her cheeks. "How do you keep getting more perfect?"

He let out a laugh. "It's a talent. I have one more thing to tell you."

She raised her eyebrows.

"I went to Derek and showed him the ring. He's

coming around to the idea of us. By the time we get married, he'll be in the wedding party. Happily."

"By the time we get married? You're assuming I'm going to say yes?" The smile teasing her mouth helped ease the butterflies in his stomach.

Him. A guy. With butterflies.

"Aren't you?" he asked.

"Yes!" she squealed and held out her left hand, wriggling her ring finger. "Assuming you ever put that gorgeous thing on me."

He plucked the ring from the velvet box and slid it onto her finger. She held up her hand, admiring the three-carat stone in a traditional platinum setting with baguettes on either side.

"There's one more thing," he said. "Something more important than the proposal or the ring."

"What's that?"

He rose to his feet and sat down beside her, cupping her face in his hand. "I love you, Nikki, and I wish I'd told you before you felt like you had to pack and leave."

She braced his face between her palms. "I love you, Asher, your grumpy moods and the happier man you show only me. And I love my ring."

He grinned. "Serenity has good taste. She helped."

"That makes it even more special." Leaning forward, she pressed her lips to his.

Need for her swelled inside him, his cock reacting, growing hard in his pants. He stripped off her clothes with more rush than finesse before pushing her onto the mattress.

Her perky breasts tempted him as he peeled off his shirt and undressed the rest of the way.

Grabbing a condom from the nightstand, he took care of protection and braced his knees on either side of her hips. "If I had patience, I'd devour you with my mouth and taste every inch of your skin."

"What will you do to me instead?" She teased him with a sassy grin.

"I need to be inside you knowing you're wearing nothing but my ring on your finger. And in case I wasn't clear, you have no idea how much I love you," he said.

At those words, she reached up, grabbed hold of his cock, and settled him at her entrance. "Asher?"

He met her gaze. "What is it, beautiful?"

"I love you, too," she said, and he thrust deep, filling her completely.

When they'd both come, her twice, they lay on the small side of the bed, the suitcase still stopping them from stretching out and really relaxing. She laid her head on his chest and breathed in and out so slowly he thought she'd fallen asleep.

As he toyed with her hair, he thought about their

story.

He'd agreed to take his friend's sister to the island for her to escape the notoriety and ended up finding the woman meant to be his.

Not a bad outcome for a simple favor, Asher thought. Not at all.

Epilogue

NO SOONER HAD Asher called his family to give them the good news about the engagement than Serenity began planning. She'd called Nikki and invited her for lunch, after which, the party was set for Labor Day weekend when it would still be warm in New York.

Gold and white balloons created arches over the pool in Harrison's backyard. He had generously donated his house for their engagement party with a little arm-twisting by Serenity. She'd promised Nikki a celebration in East Hampton, and she meant for her to have one.

Asher knew better than to get in his stepmother's way when she got into planning mode, and Nikki, never having had a true mother, let Serenity all but adopt her. Not to mention allowing her to take over the party arrangements. Serenity's work gave Nikki time to start interning with Sasha, who'd taken her on as her assistant.

K-Talent Productions was based out of the Hamptons, with an office in Manhattan, but Sasha spent most of her time out east. As a result, Nikki needed to be there learning and helping out. Within two weeks of their engagement, Asher had purchased a third home near Harrison's. It just wasn't ready for a party because it needed renovations.

He stepped outside, glad it was seventy degrees and not too warm today. The sun was a major bonus.

"People should start arriving soon," Harrison said, joining him.

"Where are the women?" Harrison hadn't been home when Asher and Nikki arrived.

He'd been at Dash Kingston's house down the road. The rock star and his family were coming to the party as he was Aurora's brother, Nick's brother-in-law. All the Kingstons were joining them.

"They're upstairs getting dressed. She's with Serenity, Jade, and her new friend, Winter. She drove in from the city with us because she needed a ride."

"Fuck me," Harrison muttered.

"What's going on with you and Winter?" Asher asked. "I assumed whatever relationship you two had ended after the interview was over?"

Harrison cleared his throat.

Before he could answer, Zach walked through the open back gate.

"Now it's a party," Zach said, walking over to them.

"How about a drink to celebrate?"

Asher glanced at his watch. "It's eleven a.m. Chill. And don't think I didn't notice you ignored that last question," he said to Harrison. "But in the spirit of the day, the caterers are going to start serving mimosas soon."

"I need something stronger," Harrison muttered, turning around, and heading back inside.

"What's going on with him?" Zach watched him go.

"Forget about it," Asher said. He already knew his brother had fucked Nikki's best friend but if he'd screwed her over, Asher would have his head.

Zach hooked an arm around Asher's neck and led him over to the bar where they shared the mimosas the staff had begun preparing. Not his first choice in alcohol but appropriate for today.

"I hear Nikki confronted her ex-friend and dirtbag boyfriend," Zach said.

Asher nodded. "They were released on bail and Nikki set up a meeting with each of them alone. She needed answers."

"You went with her, I assume?" Zach took a long sip of his drink.

"After a rip-roaring argument? Yeah. I sat at another table."

His brother let out a loud laugh. "Your girl has spunk. Did she get what she needed out of it?"

Asher nodded. "Dressed to kill in the most expensive clothes she owned and looked like a million bucks. From Meg, she heard what she'd expected. The bitch was jealous, thought she was prettier and more talented but believed Nikki used her connections to get better positions and jobs. Meg's modeling agency fired her, so she got what was coming to her. She's till trying to negotiate a deal to avoid any prison time."

"And the ex?"

Asher finished his drink and placed the glass on the bar. "The guy doesn't have half a brain. He admitted to putting the camera in Nikki's bedroom but blamed Meg for having the idea. Said it was because Nikki had slept with other photographers and men on the circuit but kept turning him down." His blood boiled at the entire thing.

Zach waved at Serenity, who'd walked outside along with their father. "So the dick was jealous."

Asher nodded. "Over nothing. Meg got him into her bed, lied to him, and convinced him to put the camera in Nikki's bedroom. She did the rest."

"People suck," Zach muttered. "But Nikki's got her whole future ahead of her. With you. So all's well that ends well." He slapped Asher on the back.

Their parents walked over. Asher hugged his father and kissed Serenity on the cheek.

Over time, the backyard began to fill up with family and friends, and he was overwhelmed with people congratulating him. There had been no debate over whether to invite her parents. She'd been firmly against it and he supported her decision. This was their day and she deserved to be surrounded by love.

Finally, his girl stepped out of the house, gorgeous in a cream-colored dress ending above her knees, her skin tanned, her straight hair falling over her shoulders. His heart swelled in his chest, knowing this beautiful woman with the kindest soul was his. For keeps.

He walked straight toward her, and not caring that she had on makeup and lipstick, he pulled her into his arms, dipped her back, and lowered his head for a long, deep kiss. Around them, the crowd burst into applause.

Thanks for reading! What's next?

What is happening between Harrison Dare and Winter Capwell?

Read JUST ONE FLING!

Revisit Dash and Cassidy in a steamy short story, JUST ANOTHER SPARK!

A surprise announcement! Are you curious to know more about Derek Bettencourt?

Erika Wilde and I are co-writing his story, JUST A LITTLE HOOK UP.

Want even more Carly books?

CARLY'S BOOKLIST by Series – visit:
https://www.carlyphillips.com/CPBooklist

Sign up for Carly's Newsletter:
https://www.carlyphillips.com/CPNewsletter

Join Carly's Corner on Facebook:
https://www.carlyphillips.com/CarlysCorner

Carly on Facebook:
https://www.carlyphillips.com/CPFanpage

Carly on Instagram:
https://www.carlyphillips.com/CPInstagram

Carly's Booklist

The Dare Series

Dare to Love Series

Book 1: Dare to Love (Ian & Riley)
Book 2: Dare to Desire (Alex & Madison)
Book 3: Dare to Touch (Dylan & Olivia)
Book 4: Dare to Hold (Scott & Meg)
Book 5: Dare to Rock (Avery & Grey)
Book 6: Dare to Take (Tyler & Ella)
A Very Dare Christmas – Short Story (Ian & Riley)

* *Sienna Dare gets together with Ethan Knight in **The Knight Brothers** (Dare Me Tonight).*

* *Jason Dare gets together with Faith in the **Sexy Series** (More Than Sexy).*

Dare NY Series (NY Dare Cousins)

Book 1: Dare to Surrender (Gabe & Isabelle)
Book 2: Dare to Submit (Decklan & Amanda)
Book 3: Dare to Seduce (Max & Lucy)

The Knight Brothers

Book 1: Take Me Again (Sebastian & Ashley)
Book 2: Take Me Down (Parker & Emily)
Book 3: Dare Me Tonight (Ethan Knight & Sienna Dare)
Novella: Take The Bride (Sierra & Ryder)
Take Me Now – Short Story (Harper & Matt)

The Sexy Series

Book 1: More Than Sexy (Jason Dare & Faith)

Book 2: Twice As Sexy (Tanner & Scarlett)

Book 3: Better Than Sexy (Landon & Vivienne)

Novella: Sexy Love (Shane & Amber)

Dare Nation

Book 1: Dare to Resist (Austin & Quinn)

Book 2: Dare to Tempt (Damon & Evie)

Book 3: Dare to Play (Jaxon & Macy)

Book 4: Dare to Stay (Brandon & Willow)

Novella: Dare to Tease (Hudson & Brianne)

* *Paul Dare's sperm donor kids*

Kingston Family

Book 1: Just One Night (Linc Kingston & Jordan Greene)

Book 2: Just One Scandal (Chloe Kingston & Beck Daniels)

Book 3: Just One Chance (Xander Kingston & Sasha Keaton)

Book 4: Just One Spark (Dash Kingston & Cassidy Forrester)

Just One Wish (Axel Forrester)

Book 5: Just One Dare (Aurora Kingston & Nick Dare)

Book 6: Just One Kiss

Book 7: Just One Taste
Book 8: Just Another Spark
Book 9: Just One Fling

For the most recent Carly books, visit CARLY'S BOOKLIST page
www.carlyphillips.com/CPBooklist

Other Indie Series

Billionaire Bad Boys
Book 1: Going Down Easy
Book 2: Going Down Hard
Book 3: Going Down Fast
Book 4: Going In Deep
Going Down Again – Short Story

Hot Heroes Series
Book 1: Touch You Now
Book 2: Hold You Now
Book 3: Need You Now
Book 4: Want You Now

Bodyguard Bad Boys
Book 1: Rock Me
Book 2: Tempt Me
Novella: His To Protect

For the most recent Carly books, visit CARLY'S BOOKLIST page
www.carlyphillips.com/CPBooklist

Carly's Originally Traditionally Published Books

Serendipity Series

Book 1: Serendipity

Book 2: Kismet

Book 3: Destiny

Book 4: Fated

Book 5: Karma

Serendipity's Finest Series

Book 1: Perfect Fit

Book 2: Perfect Fling

Book 3: Perfect Together

Book 4: Perfect Stranger

The Chandler Brothers

Book 1: The Bachelor

Book 2: The Playboy

Book 3: The Heartbreaker

Hot Zone

Book 1: Hot Stuff

Book 2: Hot Number

Book 3: Hot Item

Book 4: Hot Property

Costas Sisters

Book 1: Under the Boardwalk

Book 2: Summer of Love

Lucky Series
Book 1: Lucky Charm
Book 2: Lucky Break
Book 3: Lucky Streak

Bachelor Blogs
Book 1: Kiss Me if You Can
Book 2: Love Me If You Dare

Ty and Hunter
Book 1: Cross My Heart
Book 2: Sealed with a Kiss

Carly Classics (Unexpected Love)
Book 1: The Right Choice
Book 2: Perfect Partners
Book 3: Unexpected Chances
Book 4: Worthy of Love

Carly Classics (The Simply Series)
Book 1: Simply Sinful
Book 2: Simply Scandalous
Book 3: Simply Sensual
Book 4: Body Heat
Book 5: Simply Sexy

For the most recent Carly books, visit CARLY'S BOOKLIST page
www.carlyphillips.com/CPBooklist

Carly's Still Traditionally Published Books

Stand-Alone Books

Brazen

Secret Fantasy

Seduce Me

The Seduction

More Than Words Volume 7 – Compassion Can't Wait

Naughty Under the Mistletoe

Grey's Anatomy 101 Essay

For the most recent Carly books, visit CARLY'S BOOKLIST page

www.carlyphillips.com/CPBooklist

About the Author

NY Times, Wall Street Journal, and USA Today Bestseller, Carly Phillips is the queen of Alpha Heroes, at least according to The Harlequin Junkie Reviewer. Carly married her college sweetheart and lives in Purchase, NY along with her crazy dogs who are featured on her Facebook and Instagram pages. The author of over 75 romance novels, she has raised two incredible daughters and is now an empty nester. Carly's book, The Bachelor, was chosen by Kelly Ripa as her first romance club pick. Carly loves social media and interacting with her readers. Want to keep up with Carly? Sign up for her newsletter and receive TWO FREE books at www.carlyphillips.com.

Made in United States
North Haven, CT
20 November 2022

26992678R00173